# Likely Suspects

## by

## Barbara Jean Miller

This is a work of fiction. Names, characters, places, and incidents are either the product of the author's imagination or are used fictitiously, and any resemblance to actual persons living or dead, business establishments, events, or locales, is entirely coincidental.

**Likely Suspects**

COPYRIGHT © 2023 by Barbara Jean Miller

Cover Art by *The Wild Rose Press, Inc.*

The Wild Rose Press, Inc.
PO Box 708
Adams Basin, NY 14410-0708
Visit us at www.thewildrosepress.com

Publishing History
First Edition, 2023
Trade Paperback ISBN 978-1-5092-4965-7
Digital ISBN 978-1-5092-4966-4


Published in the United States of America

"Do you usually carry a knife in your pocket to social engagements?"

"Vincent gave me the dagger years ago, before he went off to war. He never thought we were safe, but he could do no more than that at the time."

"Thank God he was not with us."

Roslyn tilted her head at him. "But he might have helped."

"He might have been killed." Mark took a drink of brandy.

"I know it looks suspicious."

"I mean they were probably prepared to stab him to death and leave him there. They wanted all our bodies at some distance or not found at all."

She was relieved and shocked at the same time. Mark did not blame Vincent, yet had no illusions about what would have happened to them. "He will be upset."

"He is a soldier. He is used to this sort of thing."

By the time she had taped his ribs and bandaged his arm, Mark could move without grunting. She left the salve and went to her own room to lean against the closed door with a sigh. Mark was the one who was apt to be killed. Why both of them? She owned nothing, would inherit nothing. The answer came. She would have been a witness.

It was just too bad. That had been her favorite gown...because it was her only gown. At least it was not a new one, but her new slippers and stockings were ruined.

Suddenly she started laughing and slid down against the door. How inured she had become to emergencies, to weigh a new pair of slippers against her life or that of Mark.

## Praise for Barbara Jean Miller

"Ms. Miller follows in the footsteps of such genre luminaries as Mary Balogh and Mary Jo Putney to bring readers emotionally charged Regency romance."

*~Romantic Times*

## Dedication

For Dr. Ellen Spain,
who encouraged me to submit to The Wild Rose Press

Chapter One

*Glassmere, England, March, 1817*

Roslyn Clary stood staring out the drawing room window at the driving rain on the eve of yet another day with no answer. She had hoped either their brother Vincent or Mark St. John, now Lord Cahill, would respond to her letters. She was not feeling much hope but trying not to show her doubts to her sister Caroline. She leaned to get a better look down the long driveway and was rewarded with a shower of dust from the faded damask hangings.

"It has been more than two weeks. Do you think he'll come?" Caroline asked as she rubbed her abdomen while she reclined on the sofa in front of the meager fire, a lap robe thrown over her feet.

"Of course he'll come," Roslyn replied. "It would embarrass him to know we are in need. Besides, I carried the letter to the village myself this time instead of trusting someone else to mail it. It must have arrived."

"Why is he taking so long?"

"Mark St. John owns a shipping company. That is the only address I found when I searched Luther's papers. He may not even be in London."

"Oh. Should we think about packing?"

"I don't think even a St. John would evict a pregnant mother into the cold. I, on the other hand, might be

1

considered de trop."

"Roslyn, we have no place to go. Why did I marry Luther in the first place? I cannot remember."

"You mean why did you sacrifice yourself to make a home for us?" Roslyn came to take her hand. "Because you are too caring. Besides, with Father selling up the estate and moving to Bath, we had no other place to go. And ten years ago, Luther seemed tolerable."

"It's over now. Of that I can be glad."

"Perhaps there is some portion of your dowry left."

"Roslyn, please. It was very little to start with."

"I know." Roslyn sat on the stool by the sofa. "At least Luther was more addicted to dice and cards than drink. Unlike his father, he only got violently drunk on occasion."

"I had rather he drank himself to death. It would have been quicker and cheaper than being fleeced at cards by Lord Raby."

Roslyn burst out with a desperate laugh.

"Well. It's true."

"Indeed it is, but we are where we are. He was bludgeoned and left to die in the snow." Roslyn felt sad about that, but it was something she had no control over.

"Not a surprise," Caroline said, "when you consider how people hereabout thought of him."

"I wish Vincent would write. I think he left us what little money he had when he went to town to see if he could pry some funds out of the lawyers or the bank. He would not want to send us bad news, but at this point any news would be welcome." Roslyn started up at the sound of hoofbeats and ran to the window. A rider cantered up the drive, his greatcoat flapping.

"Who is it?" Caroline asked.

"Not Vincent. An express rider, I think. I shall go meet him."

"I'll stay here and await our sentence."

"Such an alarmist. Perhaps he brings money."

\*\*\*\*

Mark rode straight to the stables to get his horse under shelter as swiftly as possible. He had already stripped off the wet saddle and was rubbing Rufus down when a young groom turned out.

"Walk him up and down in the shelter of the barn until he is cool and dry. Only then feed and water him."

"Yes, sir." The lad took the reins and shuffled his feet. "Mmmm, who are you, sir?"

"Mark St. John, or perhaps Lord Cahill. I'm not quite sure. My carriage will be stopping for the night at Brixton. Should be here in the morning." He slipped the groom a coin to assure his horse would be cared for, then sprinted for the back door.

It was opened by Landis, the ancient butler, who took his greatcoat and hat. A woman came toward him down the hall that marked the short axis of the old house. She was not tall, but she carried herself as though she were. She had a paisley shawl draped about her shoulders and tied in front so that her hands were free. It was the only color in her costume, which was gray for mourning. But her burnished dark brown hair glowed in the candlclight.

Landis sighed. "Welcome home, sir, I mean, m'lord."

"No need to stand on ceremony with me, Landis."

"Do you have an express for Lady Cahill?" the woman asked as she came up with them. "I am Roslyn Clary, her sister. I will take it to her."

3

"An express?" Mark stared at the slight brown-haired girl. "No. I am Mark St. John. May I speak with both of you now?"

Her eyes widened for a second as she realized who he was.

"I see. Please come with me." She spun on her heel and preceded him down the hall to the drawing room door.

"Sorry for my late arrival, but the weather is not conducive to carriage travel."

"Which is why you finished your journey on horseback in a driving rain."

She said it over her shoulder as though it was the most normal thing for him to play vanguard to his own entourage.

He chuckled. "It was that or bear the suspense of when my carriage-sick valet would cast up his dinner all over me. I chose the night air, wet but sweet."

Miss Clary was surprised into a smile as she turned her head to look at him. She opened the door to the room herself. He saw no other servants about.

"Caroline, this is Lord Cahill."

"Lord?" he asked, casting Roslyn a worried look.

She pursed her pretty lips. "For the moment anyway."

"I think we should dispense with titles." He walked toward Lady Cahill, a widow now. She was scarcely older than her sister but blonde and fair. Her pregnancy made her look flushed and vulnerable. "After all, we are family."

"So pleased to finally meet you, sir," she whispered as she offered her hand.

"Mark St. John. Please call me Mark. He took her

4

hand briefly and insisted she not rise. "I am so sorry, but word of your loss came to my office when I was on board ship. I just got the letter today. It was from Miss Roslyn." He looked toward the sister who was watching him like a protective hawk.

"She has been better able to write what was necessary and handle matters than I."

"Of course. You are fortunate to have her with you."

Roslyn sat down on the edge of one threadbare chair. "So you have come. We should offer you condolences on the loss of your brother, as well."

Mark shrugged and seated himself. "You might if you were not aware of our estrangement. My regret has more to do with how he has left you both situated than with losing him. He didn't like me, and the feeling was mutual."

Roslyn tilted her head. "But you came anyway."

Her sister moved uncomfortably on the sofa.

"Caroline, do you wish to wait up for tea?" Roslyn asked.

"No, I truly don't. It will only keep me awake. M'lord—Mark. You may tell Roslyn whatever news you have. I am too weary to hear it."

When Mark saw she meant to rise, he took her hand and helped her up. "Shall I conduct you upstairs?"

"I will go with her. Please stay here by the fire, Mark. Perhaps you can dry your wet things."

"Rather than continuing to make a puddle on the floor," he said.

Again she smiled before she led her sister out.

"Just thought I would say what you were thinking," he mumbled.

For being sisters, the ladies were not much alike. His

sister-in-law's pregnancy would make her more vulnerable, but Roslyn looked as though she could take on an army without a second thought. Why did he like her more?

When Roslyn returned to the drawing room ten minutes later, Mark Cahill was sipping tea with his coattails to the fireplace, though the small blaze was probably not drying him much.

"I hope you don't mind. I poured."

"It's your house, for the moment."

"Of course if the child is a boy, he will be the new Lord Cahill, which is why I think we should dispense with the title for the time being."

She poured herself tea to steady her hands and wondered if he noticed there was no bread and butter or cakes. "May I ask what are your plans?" She seated herself near the tea table, but faced the fire.

"Plans? Why, to ask what are your needs. If my brother still employs old Hardwick as his man of business, I wager he hasn't given you a penny since Luther died."

"According to Mr. Hardwick, there are no pennies."

"Just as I thought, then." He pulled a jingling sack from his pocket and dropped it on the table in front of her. "I hope that is enough to take care of servants' wages and your immediate needs. The tradesmen I shall pay by check on my bank. I have already gone a round with Luther's solicitors and banker to no avail. Lady Cahill must come to London for the will to be probated."

"I suppose that must be done, though I do not know how a will can help." Roslyn stared at the purse, not daring to open it. Her hands indeed shook now as she set down her cup and saucer. "That is very generous of you.

I will see that it is dispensed."

"Am I being presumptuous in assuming you are willing to act for Lady Cahill?"

"She has not been well. Hearing business details worries and fatigues her."

"Is this the best situation for her anyway?" He glanced at the meager smoky fire and the looming windows where drafts swayed the dusty hangings. "I recall what the hall is like in winter. Would she be more comfortable in London until the weather warms?"

Roslyn bit her lip. "Caroline did ask me today if I thought we should pack."

She saw a dent appear between his brows. He seemed so self-assured she enjoyed taking him by surprise.

"Pack? To go where?"

"No idea. Frankly, after what she has been through these last ten years, she thinks you mean to put us out."

Mark choked on his tea, and his dark hair fell over his brow. "What on earth did Luther say of me that she would think such a thing?"

"He painted you very darkly." She hesitated, for she sensed they had been led astray. "Do you really want to know?"

"Perhaps not. This is your home, both of you. I have no intention of ever asking you to remove from it permanently. God knows I could never stand to live here again. But I only wondered if being near London physicians would set her mind more at rest."

"Knowing she has a roof over her head and bread on the table would set her mind at rest," Roslyn murmured. She should not be complaining to this man who was trying to help. But you never knew how hard-pressed you were until rescue arrived. Then bitterness over the shifts you had to endure sprang out.

Mark gave a slight smile. "Then by all means tell her all will be well. But ask her about London."

"I will withhold the good news till the morning. You must not be aware that your brother sold the London house."

He smiled again. "You must not be aware I have my own house in London."

"I see. So you do not expect a windfall from the estate."

"You didn't catch me with a mouthful of tea that time. I now know not to take a sip when you are talking, in case you would choke me with a riposte. I knew my brother well. I expect it will take everything I have to bring the estate back into frame for his children, whatever sex they are."

"But it is entailed. If Caroline has another girl, you will own the Hall."

"That doesn't mean I plan on living here."

He glanced around the dark room as though it was haunted. Only the small circle of light by the tea table held any cheer. "If you knew—never mind. What you don't know or I don't know matters little. Tomorrow let us make a start on repairing Luther's damage. All of his damage."

She struggled to smile and not to let any tears leak out. "Agreed."

"I'm sure Landis has made up my old room for me. I'll bid you good night and find my way."

She waited until she heard his feet on the stairs before she reached for the purse. It was full of silver, enough to pay the servants all their back wages and stock the larder as well. Mark St. John was not what she had expected. She had inferred from what he said that Luther's sole purpose in marrying and begetting children was to get an heir to push his brother Mark out permanently. That sounded like Luther.

Roslyn took charge of the purse and went upstairs to her room. She looked in on her niece Tess, but the girl was sound asleep. She thought back nine years to Tess's birth and recalled how dangerous it had been for her sister. She had to agree with Mark that London in a sound house would be a better situation for her sister, but Roslyn wondered if such a journey would be dangerous this late in her pregnancy.

As she readied herself for bed, she realized how inhospitably she had treated their rescuer. Now why was that? Possibly because she wanted to save Caroline herself. She'd have been capable of that if not for lack of funds. The small sack of silver gave her power again. Still, she must not resent Mark's efforts to rescue them, especially since she was the one who had asked to be rescued.

*****

Mark would have slept in his shirt, but Landis had laid out a nightshirt on the bed, one of Luther's, no doubt. Roslyn's letter had not said how Luther died, but Mark had no curiosity about that. He was tired. He had informed his mother, Dowager Lady Cahill, about her son's death, and she had not even blinked. She was in agreement that Caroline and Roslyn might need assistance and had made him promise to offer London as a home until the baby arrived. There could be no impediment to them staying in his house, since his mother was in residence.

He found himself fervently hoping the child would be a boy. He had never spent a happy day at Glassmere, that he recalled. His father had treated him like the runt of the litter and his brother had bullied and taunted him at every turn. Had it not been for the servants, Landis included, he would have died a hundred times over.

He suspected he now knew why they had treated him so badly, but at the time their dislike of him hurt more than the blows, more than being knocked off his horse or pushed into the lake. If his guess was correct, the reason for their contempt made it almost understandable. But he had much rather his father and brother had confronted him with the truth than just been cruel to him. He admired both the Clary ladies for being able to put up with Luther. Anything he could do to make their lives easier now was his goal, since they had faced what he could not.

Chapter Two

Roslyn rose early and went to the kitchen to pay the servants. She knew what they were owed, to the penny. There were only Landis, Cook, two maids, and one groom since the downstairs maid Molly had run off some weeks ago.

Then she went to the breakfast parlor where she sat alone over tea and toast. Landis informed her that Lord Cahill had ridden into the village at an early hour. She thought he was going to pay the tradesmen and was tempted to ask Landis if that was the case, since he knew as well as she how much was owed and to whom, but she just nodded and said nothing, as though she knew of his plans. Let Cahill take care of it if he would. She was so tired of dealing with all of them. Roslyn was vaguely aware of Cahill's carriage coming down the drive, but heard Landis usher forth, so remained seated and content.

Caroline would take a tray in her room when she woke, and Tess would eat in the nursery schoolroom with the upstairs maid. So Roslyn was alone with her thoughts, and they turned to the handsome, dark-haired St. John. He did not look or act at all like Luther. He seemed the gentleman, kind and humane. Still, how did they know they could trust him? It was simple. They had no choice.

Glassmere was nothing like she had expected when

she'd come here with Caroline. But thank God she had come, or her sister might not have survived.

Her thoughts kept wandering back to the man who wanted to forego the title and insisted they call him Mark. Beyond his physical qualities he had a sense of humor and a ready compassion. The thing was, she did not want his pity. What she did want she could not even voice. She had decided years ago to be a doting aunt and nothing more. Mark St. John stirred in her desires she thought had been put to rest long ago.

Perhaps it was the change in weather that was affecting her. She always got dismal when it rained. The sun drew out her optimistic side. Still, she had a place by Caroline's side and was teacher to Tess as well. That was her occupation. She looked for no other.

She reminded herself she did not know anything about Mark. He might be married or claimed in some other way. If not that, he would choose a London bride, especially since he had come into the title. Even if Caroline's baby was a boy, Mark would have charge of the estate for decades. And Roslyn would do what?

\*\*\*\*

Midmorning, Mark rode up the drive and around to the stable. She would have heard the hoofbeats even if she had not been watching for him. The sun was shining after the wet winter, and the grass was greening up. It took so little for hope to spring up in her soul. He had arrived in time, just in time. Before they had starved to death. He let himself in the back door with a familiarity that should offend her but which she found comforting. She went to greet him in the hall and led him to the breakfast parlor. "You have been busy today."

"Sorry, but I like an early start. I see my carriage

arrived. And my servants have probably ingratiated themselves?"

"Yes, with all the provisions they brought. All but your valet. Landis reported he stayed in the village and gave his notice."

Mark shrugged. "Small loss. I knew testing his endurance would dislodge him."

That startled a laugh from her as she sat on one of the threadbare chairs. "If you don't want a valet, why employ one?"

She was just thinking of ringing for tea when Landis and a maid came in with not only tea but eggs and ham also. They looked so proud of their efforts she smiled and thanked them. They left the door into the hall open, as was proper.

"Because a valet is expected of me, although I can't think why. My office manager engaged him. Can't a maid iron a shirt better than a man?" He went to the sideboard but came back with a plate of food for her before he served himself. She smiled and poured the tea. She had not expected a St. John to be so kind, thoughtful and, well, normal.

"I should think it is a task anyone can perform."

"And as for blacking my boots, the kitchen lad does a capital job."

Roslyn smiled at this admission. Maybe not normal but a welcome change from any gentleman she had ever met. "I'm sure he does. I paid the servants. Since I don't have to stock the larder, I can return this to you." She held out the pouch, much diminished, then took a bite of ham, suddenly feeling an appetite for it.

"Oh, keep it. Surely you, Caroline, and Tess will be needing pin money, whether you come to London or not." He laid a sheaf of papers on the table. "Receipts. Please keep those safe. And here is your mail. I thought probably you act as manager here now and can keep things in order."

"That is generous. Thank you." She took the envelopes eagerly. The letter to her father had been returned. She stared at the note from Vincent, wanting desperately to open it, but thinking that would be rude.

"Have you broached the subject of London yet?" Mark asked.

"I thought perhaps during luncheon."

"Good idea. May Tess eat with us? I have not met her yet."

"She usually does take luncheon with us, being we are so few. Here she comes now. I can tell because she jumps down the steps. Tess, say hello to your other uncle, Mark St. John. And do you want some ham and eggs?"

"Had some upstairs. What has happened?" A gangling girl with a dowdy blue dress and a freckled nose matching her red hair came and curtsied in front of him.

"How do you do, sir?"

"Very well, and you?"

"Terrible. The storm kept me awake."

"Well, it's moved off, and we have the sun back."

"I used to have a pony to ride."

Mark smiled. "Perhaps you'll have one again."

"His name was Wembley."

"What will you name the next one?"

Tess squinted her eyes. "I'd have to see it first."

"I can see where this is going," Roslyn said. "We can't get a pony just now."

Tess fell silent and sat on the very edge of a chair. It pained Roslyn to rain on their discourse, but they could not drag a pony to London or even drag one back from London.

"You are probably waiting for your sister to come down. How about Tess showing me the grounds? I have not been here since I was child myself. Much could have changed."

"If you would not be bored."

"I would be delighted," he said.

Tess leaped off the chair and took his hand. He expected her to make for the back door and the stable. This proved to be a good assumption.

She went down the row of stalls, admiring his team and riding horse but also telling him what horses and ponies had occupied the stalls before, as though he could put all of them back. He fervently wished he had been part of Tess's life before this, but that did not mean he could have prevented any disasters.

Next they visited the garden, which was empty this time of year except for a row of Brussels sprouts staggering sideways like drunken soldiers now that most of their little heads had been harvested.

She showed him the empty chicken house where there were no longer chickens and, saddest of all, Hoppy and Thumper's pen where her rabbits used to live. He could only think that the animals had been slaughtered for food. He was making a mental list of all the things he now felt he owed this poor child.

Lastly she took him to the willow tree by the stream and showed him her secret hideaway. A combination of tall grasses and overhanging limbs must provide an almost rainproof shelter in the summer, but today the sun glinted through the limbs and sent a pattern of beams across the grass under the tree. The bench under the overhanging limbs was not dry, so they did not tarry except to sail dried oak leaves into the stream like little boats. He was especially sad that this little girl had not a better childhood. It had not been as bad as his, but it was far from happy.

Mark and Tess came back in, not much muddied, and Roslyn met them in the hall. Caroline came downstairs then with a bright smile and an easy grace in spite of her pregnancy. The easing of her cares had worked wonders. "I see you've met Tess."

Mark took Caroline's hand. "We've been discussing the merits of ponies."

"Ponies are all we discuss at some meals, but let's not for today, all right?" She stroked Tess's hair, then walked with Mark into the dining room.

Roslyn pulled her letter from her pocket and tore open Vincent's note. Briefly it said Vincent could make no headway, but would borrow some money to tide them over. She folded up the note. So he had failed. She felt worse for her brother than for herself. She would send a letter today telling him of their rescue. How to write it without making him feel a failure would be a challenge.

After Landis brought the beef stew, they ate for a few moments while Mark composed his speech. The meal was less spartan than last night's tea, probably thanks to the box of provisions he had made up at home before leaving. There were turnips and carrots, not buttered but spiced with some herb that made them appetizing. Dried apples had been stewed with a bit of honey. Mark fancied himself better pleased with the meal than either Caroline or Roslyn appeared to think he would be.

"I'm sure you are used to better fare," Caroline

apologized.

"Even the owner of ships has to subsist on salted beef and cooked pea porridge during a voyage. I am well content. Please send my compliments to your cook. What took me so long in the village was my visit to Mr. Hardwick. I hope it was not forward of me to approach him, but he didn't give a good rendering of accounts when surprised like that, which was my intent. In fact he could not or would not give me the account books."

"You suspect him of carelessness?" Caroline asked.

"I suspect him of embezzlement. If he can produce the account books, I will take them to my assistant in London to go over. If not, I am giving him the boot. I am inclined to anyway. He never spared a thought for all of you."

"Whatever you think is best," Caroline said, blue eyes gazing raptly with wonder.

Roslyn supposed Caroline could never dismiss anyone, even with just cause. For her part, she would like to do far worse to Hardwick than send him packing.

"What I think is that the estate can support you eventually, but we may need new management."

"He made us sell our horses and *my* pony." Tess sent Mark an accusing look.

"That settles it. Hardwick goes. 'Tis a day for being decisive." He got a smile from Tess, then sent Roslyn a speaking look.

She cleared her throat to avoid the smile that threatened to peek through. "Mark, I mean, Lord Cahill, was wondering if we, all of us, would like to go to London, at least until the baby is born." She looked up to see Caroline staring at her as though she had run mad.

"It is still very cold here, and London would be

festive and comfortable. You could come back in the summer. What do you say?" Mark looked so expectantly at Caroline that Roslyn wanted to answer for her sister.

Caroline tried to speak but had to clear her throat first. "Would a gentleman's house be able to accommodate the three of us and two maids?"

"Gentleman's house? I assure you my house may be in Southwark, but it is large, and Mother has already planned what rooms you are to have."

"Whose mother?" Roslyn asked.

"My mother, Elizabeth St. John."

Caroline stared at him. "But your mother is dead. The old Lord Cahill told us so."

Mark dropped his fork. "I assure you she is quite alive. Perhaps he meant she was dead to him."

"May I be excused?" Tess asked.

Caroline smiled at Tess. "Of course, dear."

"I am going to play in the stable." She said it like a threat.

"Don't get underfoot," Caroline said absently. "My late husband seemed to be in agreement. In fact he said you killed her."

Mark choked and dropped his water glass onto the table with a thunk but did not overturn it. "You both seem to have a knack for conversational clinkers."

"Why did he lie to us?" Roslyn asked of her sister.

Mark shook his head as though to get some sense out of the misunderstanding. "How did he explain the lack of a funeral or a notice in the *Times?*"

"I was confined with Tess. I suppose I didn't notice the lack of those things."

Roslyn shook her head. "And I had no reason in those days to disbelieve him."

"I assure you, Mother is alive and well. She truly wants you to visit. She is already interviewing London practitioners. But first, is it safe for you to travel?"

"Oh, I am fine. I probably have another three weeks. But London! I thought never to see it again."

"Not that we would be going about," Roslyn said.

"Why not, if Caroline is feeling well. And Mother receives many guests at the house. Her dinner parties are quite the thing."

"What do you say?" Roslyn asked.

Caroline smiled suddenly, and it was like a ray of sunshine in a gray day. "I say let's pack." Caroline talked then of London and her come-out season, and Mark responded politely. But Roslyn had not been there and was left out of the reminiscence. Once Caroline realized this, she stopped. "That was all so long ago."

"I'm back," Tess announced. "If your horses are not going to stay here, there is plenty of room for ponies."

"Tess, we are going to London." Caroline hugged her. "You will get to see so much."

"Do they have ponies there?"

Mark nodded. "Lots."

****

When he was in the village, Mark had tried to see the magistrate and was told the man would be available at two o'clock, so he was planning on riding back there after lunch. He and the ladies had no more finished eating than Landis announced the arrival of Magistrate Lowry and Doctor Benson.

Mark went to the morning room, where they had been shown. He would have to prod the servants to light a fire in more than one room, or the ladies would be deprived of their work space for the length of the

19

interview.

"Lord Cahill. I am Magistrate Lowry. This is Doctor Benson. I hope we are not intruding."

"You are most welcome. Pleased to meet both of you." For once Mark did not disclaim the title as he shook hands. "Please have a seat."

"Sir James Hardwick told me you had come to him and demanded an accounting of his work."

"Is Hardwick complaining of my request to see the books?"

"Yes, until I told him you were within your rights as Lord Cahill."

"A temporary title, perhaps, since Caroline is about to deliver a child. At least we all hope the baby is a son. Let me get you each a brandy against the chill."

Both men smiled and nodded as they seated themselves. "How is she?" the doctor asked.

"Seems blooming, now there is food on the table. Hardwick is a thief, and I plan to prove it."

"That may be, but it isn't what I thought you wanted to discuss." Lowry cleared his throat.

Mark handed them each a small glass of spirits he hoped was adequate.

"What then?

"Your brother's murder."

Mark bobbled the brandy decanter and nearly dropped it.

"Murder? No one said anything to me about murder."

"He was found in the freezing cold by a carter, bludgeoned," the magistrate said.

The doctor nodded. "He died next day in his bed."

"But what was he doing out in such weather?"

"No one knows. I talked to all the tenants and servants. All were indoors." The doctor sipped his drink.

Lowry finished his brandy. "The inquest brought in a verdict of murder by person or persons unknown."

"Does Caroline know?"

"She knew there was an inquest, but Miss Clary went in her stead. Obviously Lady Cahill was not about in such weather. In fact, the women slept together that night for safety. Lord Cahill and his guest had been drinking, so Miss Clary stayed with her sister."

"What do we do now?" Mark asked.

"Nothing, as far as I can see." The magistrate shook his head. "We have no witnesses, no weapon."

"You are sure it could not have been an accident?"

Lowry shook his head. "He was not much liked hereabouts. Murder seems the likely conclusion."

"So the blow killed him, not the cold?"

"No, the blow to the back of the head bled profusely and left him unconscious," the doctor replied. "But he died of exposure."

"Still, it was murder," the magistrate insisted.

"Where was Hardwick that night?"

"He claims to have been in London. There was a guest here, Lord Raby. He says he heard nothing. I interviewed everyone on the estate who might have had a reason to kill Cahill."

Mark shook his head. "Which apparently would be all of them."

"Unfortunately. It took some time. I also talked to some of the tradesmen. Not a lot of sympathy there. I tell you this for your own safety and that of the ladies."

"Thank you for telling me, but why would we be in danger?"

"We do not know why he was killed. If it was for the estate, even the unborn babe could be at risk." Lowry gave Mark a hard stare.

"Doctor, the ladies wish to remove to London until summer. Do you consider it safe for Lady Cahill to travel?"

"If the carriage is well sprung and the journey made at a moderate pace, yes."

"Thank you. I think they need to be where it is warmer for a time."

"And safer," the magistrate said.

"You really fear for them?"

"Since someone murdered your brother, they may not be safe anywhere."

"But the only one with a motive—oh, I see. You suspect me."

"Of course not. You were at sea, were you not?"

"Yes, my ship returned two days ago. Do you know of anyone who would benefit by Luther's death except Hardwick, who must fear exposure?"

"Oh, not more than half the county."

Mark sighed. "Yes, he owed everyone who sold any goods or services. Forcing the estate to be settled would at least pay the debts. I paid off all the merchants I could think of, but there are surely others. If you hear of any, send them to me."

The doctor placed his glass on the piecrust table and made a negative motion when Mark offered to refill it. "It made me think back to your father's death. I thought poison at the time, but he was a heavy drinker."

Mark sat down. "You're suggesting someone wants to eliminate our entire family?"

"What happens to the estate then?" the magistrate

asked.

"I'd have to ask the solicitor. If there are no distant relatives…but there must be someone."

"I leave that for you to investigate. The responsibility for Lady Cahill is now on you."

After they left, Mark sat a long time, thinking over the conflicts his father had set in motion and the character his father's meanness had fostered in Luther. He got out pen and ink to make a list of neighbors and townsfolk he remembered his father or brother had offended or cheated. It was a long list. Then he called Landis.

The man stood at attention, and Mark smiled to try to relieve the old servant's mind.

"As this is likely to be a long conversation, will you sit?"

"I could not, m'lord."

"Then I shall stand. The inquest, were you there?"

"I was called to give evidence, m'lord."

"What evidence?"

"That your brother left sometime in the small hours and the back door remained unlocked. I did not sit up, since this was not an unusual happening."

"He never returned."

"He was found several miles away, not far from the church. If I had looked for him I would not have looked there."

"No, do not blame yourself. I would never have looked there either."

"I planned to canvas the roads and inns the next day. He was found, almost buried in snow, by a carter."

"Did Lady Caroline know the verdict?"

"She was prostrate. Miss Clary came in her stead

and may have told her the verdict later, or she may have decided to shield her from it."

"I see. The doctor has raised the question of my father's death being intentional as well."

Landis staggered a step sideways. "That was the verdict for your brother, murder."

"Yes, Father was not well liked either. Could you look over this list of likely suspects and see if anyone leaps out at you for either death?" Mark handed him the page.

Landis carried the list to the desk, and while standing took up the pen and crossed out several. He glanced up at Mark. "Deceased." He then added an alarming number of names and made some other marks. "I have annotated whether the quarrel was with your father, your brother, or both."

Mark took the list from him and shook his head. "When I left, I thought never to have to deal with something like this. Do you and the staff feel safe here?"

"Yes, of course. You will be taking the nursery maid and the lady's maid with you? That leaves only the groom, Cook, and me."

"Don't you have a downstairs maid?"

"Molly Wells disappeared the night of your brother's death. Her family says they do not know where she is."

"Wells, the blacksmith?"

"I added his name since he has not been paid in some time. Also because of his missing daughter, for which he blames us."

"I missed him on my rounds. I'll go see him today."

"Pardon my saying this, but it might be better if I paid him."

"Why?" Mark stared at the old retainer.

"He does need the money, but I'm sure he would throw it back in your face."

"Yes, of course. I am leaving you with a sum to maintain the house while the ladies are away." Mark handed over a pouch of silver. "I plan to make Hardwick surrender the estate books. He is not permitted to handle any more estate business."

"You sacked him, sir?" Landis asked with a smile.

"Yes. You are in charge here for the time being. No decisions need be made about crops for a few months anyway. Anything else?"

"We have recovered the old cart pony you asked for, but if Miss Tess sees it, she may not want to leave."

"Still, it would set her mind at rest. I will go and get her."

Mark found the child doing lessons in the chilly schoolroom, which looked like an abandoned crypt with its dusty and broken toys.

"May I interrupt?"

Roslyn smiled up at him. "We are finished for today. So hard for either of us to concentrate when all we can think of is London."

"Look at this map of the city. Look how big it is," Tess said.

"It would be easy for you to get lost in London, so you are to always be with one of us, all right?"

"Can we look for a pony there?"

"Maybe a younger one, but for now come say hello to an old one."

"You found him?" Tess jumped up and down, clapping her hands. Then she rushed out of the room. When Mark and Roslyn got to the stable, she was already grooming the old pony as he ate some grain.

"He's so thin."

"He will gain all his weight back by summer when we return."

"I know we have to leave him. He cannot walk that far. Roddy will take care of him, won't you?"

The stable lad smiled. "I promise, Miss Tess."

"Maybe when I come back I will bring him a companion."

Mark chuckled. "I would not be a bit surprised."

Chapter Three

Mark looked across the carriage at Roslyn. "I was hoping they would both sleep away the journey."

She glanced at her sister reclining on a bank of pillows in one corner of the carriage. It was rather pleasant to have someone fussing over them and seeing to their needs besides her. Not that she did not like to take care of them, but she was without the resources to do so properly. It felt good to have Mark also be concerned for her welfare. He seemed a longsuffering man, for Tess was leaning against his side. "Tess is wrinkling your coat."

"She's as light as a feather. Did Luther ever do anything to her? I mean how did Tess regard her father?"

"He barely noticed her most of the time. But he never guarded his tongue around her and frightened her when he did go looking for her. For Christmas she wanted a pet, anything to replace the pony."

"What did he get her?"

"A fur muff made of the finest dead rabbit skin."

"Oh, God!"

"He thought it an excellent substitute. He did not study to be mean to her; he was just inept."

"But he wanted a son. Who bought her the pony?"

"No one. It was a cart pony that could no longer pull the cart. I started leading her on it, and she got the poor old thing to move when no one else could. Eventually she was able to ride about on him bareback. Then that awful agent sold everything. The pony could not have been worth much. For Tess it was tragic."

"Roddy will see it is waiting for her when we get back to Glassmere. I'm sure she cried more over losing it than over her father."

She stared at him. "None of us cried over Luther. I am sorry, but I had to say that. Caroline was prostrate because she did not know what would become of us. Luther's death was a blessing."

"I did know him to be a bad man, but I assume I did not see him at his worst."

"No, you could not have. He was not horrible at first, not till Tess was born and there were no pregnancies after that for years. When we get home again, it will be a pleasanter home to return to. I have been thinking we need some time away from it to expunge the bitter memories of all that has happened there. We will view it differently in the summer after a few months' absence."

"Assuming you don't capture the attentions of the *ton* and find yourself betrothed in the next few months."

"I have no intention of marrying."

He stared at her in surprise at this rehearsed speech. "Ever?"

"Never."

"Why ever not?"

"The examples of marriage I have seen are nothing to entice me. Luther gambled away every penny once he became a lord. Before that, we had your father drinking himself to death. Never mind the rest. I will never put myself under the power of a man again."

Mark decided not to argue with her and had a clever thought. "I feel the same way about marriage."

"You do?" Roslyn looked surprised.

"I'm simply not good husband material, always at work or off on a voyage. I don't think I would be good at it."

Roslyn glanced at Tess snuggling against his side. "Perhaps you underrate yourself. If you don't mind my asking, how did your mother come to be with you?"

"My assistant, Thomas Winslow, managed it. I left home at twenty and took a post on a cargo vessel bound for America. I found a mentor in Boston who taught me navigation and let me trade as his agent until I could afford a ship of my own. Within three years I could afford a house, so I sent my schoolmate Thomas to Landis with a letter telling him to ask Mother to come to London. Thomas was still admitted at the estate because he took money to her, money which Luther hoped to snatch from her. Luther and Father rode off to the village to buy brandy, and Landis helped her and her maid pack. Landis told everyone she was going on a visit."

"Courageous of him. He might have been dismissed."

"He knew where to find us if that happened. Even though my house is in Southwark, Mother can invite her old friends to our place."

"How awful for them to tell us she was dead. But we never get any news here. Even the mail is usually picked up by Hardwick. If we get any letters, we never see them. Our brother Vincent wrote that he has made no headway with the lawyers. That was the first mail we have had in years."

"Where is he now?"

"Other than London, I do not know. He put no return direction on his note."

"Hardwick has a lot to answer for."

"We have been very much prisoners."

"That is at an end. Mother's one regret is that she was not here to buffer Caroline from Luther, but she had no control over him or Father, who only wanted her portion and cared nothing for her."

"Just as Luther wanted Caroline's dowry."

"She was lucky to have you. I think you may have saved her life. I shall try to make that up to both of you."

Caroline finally woke around noon, so Mark had them stop at the next inn to change horses and ordered soup and bread for them. Roslyn had to pinch herself to think that any man could be so courteous and thoughtful. Tess was enthralled with the hens and geese in the yard such that she hardly ate. Roslyn caught Mark stashing an apple in his coat pocket which he would probably produce later for Tess.

When they got closer to town, Tess unrolled the map of London she had been studying earlier, and Mark could point at each of many landmarks and relate some incident that happened there, not always to his credit. They laughed much for an hour. When asked if they wanted to stop for dinner or push on, they all voted to finish the trip that day. Both fell asleep again, and Roslyn looked tensely out the window.

"Still holding your breath?" he asked. "I hope we have left any violence behind us."

"Now that Luther is dead. The magistrate still holds that he was murdered? Is that why he came to see you?"

"Yes. Luther was greatly disliked by many people. I made a list, but most of his quarrels hardly seem motives for murder."

"A list of suspects?"

"Yes, apparently the magistrate thinks I should solve this mystery from a distance, though he has made no headway. Probably wanted to give the culprit a medal."

Roslyn sighed. "I had thought it might be Wells, the blacksmith."

Mark recalled Landis's reaction to Wells. "Why?"

"His daughter disappeared that night. In fact, I lived in fear that she would turn up dead."

"Oh, at Luther's hand?"

"He pressed his attentions on her."

"You did not tell them this at the inquest?"

"No, for I had no proof, nor any reason to ruin any more lives."

Mark weighed in his mind if a strong man would be angry enough to strike the fatal blow knowing his daughter was at risk. He decided yes, and that he would not blame him. He would do so himself. "I'm sorry I did not come sooner."

"Two months matters little."

He shook his head. "Years ago would have been better. Perhaps I could have helped somehow."

"You had no right to interfere. The odd thing is that Luther was all right in the beginning. He did not even cavil at supporting me. It was not a love match, but Caroline did not mind him. He was fun and laughed a lot, but with the years adding up and no son, he grew bitter."

"But he did not take it out on Tess, did he?"

"He seldom spoke to her, so she came to avoid him as though she had done something wrong."

"And you could not make her believe it was not her fault."

"She has spunk. She stood up to Raby, but Luther saddened her. Also, we got letters those early years, from my mother and our friends. Those seemed to stop quite suddenly, even though we still wrote."

"Hardwick. How evil to deprive you of something that could not profit him."

"I knew for certain when I upturned the tall vase in the hall. I used to throw pennies in there in case Tess needed anything. When I dumped it out, our letters to everyone were in there, never posted."

"That had to be Luther. That is criminal."

"A good thing I did not find them until he was dead or I would have made him pay."

"Your sister and Tess were lucky to have you as their champion."

"As soon as we reach London, I plan to write to everyone."

Mark was amazed she still had hope after all she had been through. "Good idea. Let them know you are back in the world again." He watched her take a deep breath and press her lips as though fighting tears.

"I don't understand why the lack of a son would change him so much."

"You always hope that if someone changes dramatically, it will be for the better."

"That was not the case," she said.

"Well if he *was* murdered, he paid the price for his sins. Let's not speak of him again."

"You are nothing like him."

"Thank you."

They did not arrive in London till after dark. His butler, Meason, opened the door, and Mark's mother was waiting in the hall. "Lady Elizabeth St. John, may I present Lady Caroline St. John, Miss Roslyn Clary, and of course Tess St. John.

"There you are, you precious girls. Your rooms are ready for you, and dinner will be at your convenience."

"Oh, I am still full from lunch," Caroline said. "Would anyone mind if I went to bed?"

"Of course not, dear. Mark, you amuse Tess while Roslyn and I help Caroline upstairs."

"Let's go to the library. You might like the books or the globe."

When Mark set the branch of candles on the large desk, Tess twirled to look around the room at the towering shelves. Then she spied the globe, which was almost as tall as she, and ran to it. Mark obligingly held the candelabra while she spun it and stopped it with her finger on Madagascar.

"Have you been here?"

"Not yet. Mostly I run between Charleston, Philadelphia, Boston, and London, though I do go to the continent on occasion." He pointed out France and Spain on the globe, then Africa. "Very tame, I assure you. We deliver manufactured goods and take away china, rice, rum, lumber, and fruit."

"Wembley looked glad to see me."

"They will take good care of him until you return. Of course, you will need a younger mount for town."

She clasped her hands together. "Another pony?"

"Since you are almost ten already, you will quickly outgrow a pony. I think we should search for a little mare for you. Once we are settled, Roslyn can help us look for one. Tattersalls is the place to look, and the next sale is Thursday."

When Roslyn was shown into the library, she was awed by the collections of books now available to them.

Mark saw her gazing around the room in wonder.

"Don't credit me with finding them all. They came with the house, which I bought from an elderly recluse. I wish I had known him in life. We have the same tastes in literature."

"Except you are not a recluse."

"No, but I cannot think why else he planted his house in the middle of a nine-acre square of lots unless he had plans for a very large garden."

"That is a lot of land in the city, but Tess does like to roam. It will be so much easier to give Tess lessons here."

"Look at the globe." Tess ran to it and pointed to England. "We are right here."

"I see it."

"And tomorrow we search for a horse, not a pony."

"On the day after tomorrow," Mark corrected. "Thursday."

Roslyn sent him a withering look.

"A small horse, not much bigger than a pony." Mark made compacting motions with his hands to quell her disapproval.

"You will spoil her," Roslyn whispered.

"What harm to indulge her since she has had so little all these years?"

Tess was allowed to dine with them since it was just the four of them. She entertained her grandmother with an account of the trip and the sights they planned to see. She went from babbling energy to a fatigue so profound she nearly fell asleep in her chair.

"Shall I carry her up?" Mark offered.

"No, she can still walk if I guide her." Roslyn roused Tess and marched her toward the stairs.

His mother Elizabeth smiled on both of them. "We

will have tea in the drawing room directly, if you care to come back down."

"I would like that very much."

When Roslyn came down, she went straight to Elizabeth. The older woman had white hair and merry blue eyes, the image of a perfect grandmother, and now Tess was her grandchild. Of course she would be happy.

"Thank you so much for having us. I think we were all under a strain at Glassmere, and exhaustion is a sign of it."

"Please sit, and call me Aunt Beth. It was not the journey? Mark is known for pushing his horses." She handed Roslyn a cup of tea with cream and sugar.

"Not at all. He took very good care of us. I have only now realized that one does not react to stress or fear until they are removed. Then one sees how close to the edge one was."

"If only we had known. But we have both been persona non grata there for years."

Mark took a cup of tea from his mother. "And the only address you had was the shipping company."

"Yes, since the London town house was sold, we had no idea how else to reach you."

"The town house has not been sold," Elizabeth said.

"But Luther said it was."

"When I was shopping, just today, I saw Mr. Hardwick knocking at the front door." Elizabeth frowned at the remembrance. "I called to him, but either he didn't hear or he ignored me."

Mark blew out a tired breath. "I suppose I had better nip over there first thing and get the locks changed so he doesn't sell the furniture out of the place. Mother, I discharged Hardwick before we left. I wonder why he scrambled to town so fast."

"I never liked the man." His mother gave a juvenile pout that made him laugh.

Roslyn frowned. "Why would Luther lie about that?"

"So he would not have to bring Caroline to town," the elder Lady Cahill said.

"I see. He was far worse than I thought, then." Roslyn bit her lip. "I'm sorry. He was your son."

"I disowned him long ago. He was very much like his father."

"I am more like Mother," Mark said with a satisfied smile.

"Which is to say you are sane and decent." His mother looked him up and down.

Mark choked on his tea. "I should be used to plain-speaking women, but one of you will be the death of me. So our list for this week includes securing the town house and finding a mare for Tess."

"I have invited a physician for Caroline to interview but not until afternoon. There are many in the city. She need not take the first one."

"No Thomas at dinner tonight," Mark said, "and no stack of paperwork. I should catch up with him in the morning so he does not think I have been murdered."

"Why ever would he think that?" Elizabeth asked.

Mark cleared his throat. "The magistrate seems to think Luther was murdered."

"Is that true?" she asked Roslyn.

"I don't know. He suffered a blow to the head."

"But died of exposure," Mark added.

Elizabeth looked taken aback, but Roslyn could think of no way to soften the blow. "I think because he was so unpopular they thought the chances were it was murder."

"I would not be surprised. Who do they think did it?"

"There seems to be an embarrassment of suspects." Mark unfurled the list from his pocket, causing his mother to curse lightly under her breath as she reached for her spectacles.

"Let me see."

He moved to stand over her.

"But this is nearly everyone in the district."

"I know, and I got the notion the magistrate had no intention of investigating further."

"So why even talk to you?"

"Once he ascertained I could not have done it to get the title, he seemed to think we might all be in danger from some distant heir. Have we got one, someone who would inherit if Caroline's child is a girl and I am out of the way?"

"Don't even say such a thing."

"He asked, and I did not know."

"We don't dwell much on family history, and I do not know my side of the family all that well. Your father had no brothers, but he had cousins. I will look into it." She turned her attentions back to Roslyn. "How horrible for you, child, to be planted in such a family."

"I was just thinking you should add my name to the list."

"What?" squeaked Mark.

"I am the one who sent him to the church."

The older lady arched an eyebrow. "If you got Luther to go near a church, more power to you."

"He came to my room and demanded to see

Caroline. I told him she was praying for his soul."

"He really thought she would go out in such weather?" Mark asked.

"He was very drunk."

"You have been the protector of Caroline and Tess all these years," Mark said. "You could not have been much more than a child yourself when she married."

"I was glad to be with her."

Mark's mother smiled at her. "Now you are here and can stand down from your duties for a bit and have some fun."

"I don't think I can, you know. When one has been on guard as long as I have, relaxing seems so abnormal there is no comfort in it. I will leave you now with the hope that Tess sleeps late so you can do what you need to about the house without her plaguing you."

Mark understood what she was saying but hoped her habit of duty would not last forever. He wanted to see Roslyn smiling and dancing, caring for nothing but music and fashionable dresses. He also knew such a transformation would be false. If she managed to appear that way, it would be an act. Her suspicion of the world and its evils would remain. If he could not manage to make her happy, he must contrive to at least make her feel safe. He had to find Luther's killer and make sure no one was out to get the rest of them.

Chapter Four

Mark was up before first light, having tea and toast in the library while he went over the papers Thomas had brought home from the office the previous night. He was glad for the impulse that had made him offer his business manager a room at the house rather than lodgings in a sometimes dangerous town. Besides, Thomas made his mother laugh and gave a family feel to the dinner table when he was there.

Mark did not leave the house until after seven, while all were still asleep. First he rode toward the Cahill townhouse in Mayfair. It was not close, so winding his way through Southwark and crossing London Bridge was enough of a ride to get his brain going. He was reviewing the list of suspects in his head when the jingle of a bridle and striking of iron shoes almost next to him caused him to jerk the reins, almost sending his mount into the bridge railing.

A rider swung something at him and slashed him across the back. If Mark had not slid sideways he might have been knocked off his horse. Then he felt it, a sharp pain in his shoulder blade and a trickle of blood. Once his horse got its bearings and he righted himself, he looked after the fellow, but the rider had galloped away and turned right at the end of the bridge. Mark halted his horse and pushed his wadded handkerchief inside his coat over the wound. The coat was tight enough to keep the cut compressed.

As his heart returned to a more normal beat, he speculated on who wanted him dead, for the blow had been meant to send him into the Thames. He did not think Hardwick rode well enough to pull such a stunt. Of course, he could have hired someone. Mark looked around, but no one else was about. He might have died on the bridge or fallen in the river and no one would have known what had happened to him. He had felt alone before, when he had escaped to America with little in the way of hope, but he had never before felt so absolutely powerless.

Working his way through Mayfair seemed tame compared to the immediate encounter. Perhaps the magistrate was right about heirs to the estate being in danger. There was no knocker on the front door of the Cahill townhouse, and when he did knock he did not raise anyone. He took the keys his mother had still had in her possession and went around back. He let his horse into the stable, where there already resided a warhorse and a cover hack, and then approached the kitchen. There was a scent of coffee and bacon when he knocked at the back entrance. A man in shirtsleeves and a coarse apron answered.

"I am Lord Cahill," Mark said reluctantly.

"Do you wish to see Captain Clary?"

"Vincent Clary? Yes."

The man took his hat and gloves and showed him into the breakfast parlor, where a wiry man a decade older than Mark was consuming a meager meal and reading the *Times*, from which he finally looked up. "Who let you in?"

"Your man."

"I'd share with you, but…"

"I already breakfasted." Mark seated himself and took a breath. "Is it true that Hardwick came here yesterday?"

"He tried to get in, but Evers threw him out," Vincent said before returning his attention to the *Times*.

"Good, because I have sacked Hardwick. He refuses to turn over the estate ledgers. I will also bring an action against him."

"He cannot turn them over."

"Because he did not keep any?"

Vincent looked up from his paper finally, his gray eyes steely with resentment. "No, because I stole them."

Mark let an uncontrollable laugh bubble up. "From his office?"

"No, from the estate office at Glassmere. He always locked them up there after he worked on them. I sprang the lock and took them with me the last time I was there. At least he no longer resided there. Even Luther could not stomach him all day long."

"Would that be the night Luther died?"

"No, I was not there that night, but have visited since to see how my sisters and niece go on. The magistrate seemed to think I killed Luther. Do you?"

Mark smiled. "The magistrate thinks any number of people are suspects. It is a popular club. And what did you find out from the ledgers?"

"I can count cards, but I am not an accountant. I think he listed goods my sisters never got. Beyond that, I do not know, except that the solicitors and the bank will not advance any money for them to live on."

"My mother is caring for them at our house in town. Will you give the ledgers to me so I can have my assistant audit them? He would have a better chance of finding irregularities than either of us."

"Why not? Wait right here." Vincent rose and strode off into what Mark recalled was the morning room.

In the time Vincent was gone, his man served Mark a cup of black coffee and Mark thanked him. Evers hesitated behind him.

"Sir, ye have a saber slash on the back of yer coat."

"Yes, I know."

The man gave a chuckle and left.

Vincent returned with a saddle bag containing three large ledgers. He too hesitated behind Mark before he dumped the satchel on the chair next to him. "What now? Shall I pack my meager belongings and leave?"

Mark looked up at him. "Why?"

"Because this is not my house. It is yours."

"It belongs to Caroline, and I think she might feel comfortable having you look after it. Better than having Hardwick in here carrying off the furniture."

"You mean I may stay?" Vincent asked in surprise.

"I want you to stay, but you really need more staff to perhaps…dust." He ran a finger along a chair back. "And take care of the stable. I shall leave you with some temporary funds for upkeep here." He reached into his pocket and made a neat stack of sovereigns on the bare table.

"Why?" Vincent shook his head, the noticeable dents between his eyebrows pronounced and his ash-blond hair curling over his brow.

"I have brought Caroline, Tess, and Roslyn up to town to stay with my mother so they can be more comfortable for the birth of the babe. Also, there can be no probate without Caroline present. Now the solicitors have no reason to delay."

"But if it is a boy, he is the new Lord Cahill."

Mark stretched his legs out in front of him but remembered not to lean back. "That is my sincerest hope. In any case, we should probably all share guardianship of the child, especially if Luther *was* murdered."

"Are you serious? Why would you trust me?" Vincent looked utterly confused.

"You are her brother, and I do not know you well enough not to trust you."

Mark watched as Vincent must have been weighing this statement in his mind.

Then Vincent laughed outright and sat down. "Seriously, Caroline might only regard me as a bad influence."

Mark winced as he turned to look at the ledgers. "At least you were there for her when I was not."

"I thought if I was at Glassmere, I could keep anything dreadful from happening to them, but I could not."

Mark glanced at him. "I don't think losing Luther was that dreadful for her."

"Then there is Lord Raby to worry about. He is after Roslyn."

"I see." Mark now gave Vincent his full attention. "We shall have to be on guard against him."

"You should not admit the fellow to your house. I know I played cards with them. I won what I could from Luther to keep Raby from getting it all. But I could not really help them."

"Do you think Raby could have killed Luther?"

"Why would he? Luther owed him money."

"Perhaps the whole village got together and

bludgeoned my brother, but then he would have had more than one head wound, or possibly no head."

Vincent laughed finally and stood. "Are you aware your shoulder is bleeding? Saw it when I came back in."

"Yes, that is one of the reasons I want you as a joint guardian."

Vincent's smile slid away to a look of genuine concern. "Someone tried to kill you?"

"Someone almost succeeded," Mark said, standing and weighing the satchel on his injured right side, then shifting it to his left arm. "Get your man to victual the larder. He was your batman during the war, was he not?"

"How did you know that?"

"The coffee, and he still calls you 'Captain.' Also, he is good at living on a thread with elegance, as you are."

Vincent looked at the coins piled on the table as though they were an illusion. "Why are you doing this?"

"To keep the place safe for the boy we hope for and to make sure he has two uncles rather than one. Here is my direction." Mark handed over his card. "Please call on your sisters and niece."

"Are you sure they would want to see me? I feel I have failed them."

"You are their only close family, are you not?"

Vincent took a breath. "We used to be close."

"They need you now more than ever, if someone is indeed bent on wresting the title away from a child yet unborn."

"You take this threat to be against the whole family?"

"Anyone in possession of the title."

When he walked out the door and toward the back

of the house, Evers offered to carry the saddle bags and load them on his horse.

"Much appreciated." In the stable he said, "Hold the fort here, Evers."

Belatedly he wondered if he should have asked Evers to tend the wound, but it seemed to have stopped bleeding, so maybe it was nothing serious.

Mark left the shipping orders at the office with the warehouse manager, then rode toward home. By the time he returned to the house he was feeling dizzy. The cut had opened again when he dismounted from his hack. He wanted nothing more than to retreat to his room and check the damages, but his assistant Thomas was there in the hallway.

"I really need you to look at these contracts." The businesslike Thomas wore spectacles and a neat brown suit.

"And I really need you to look at these books." He thrust the satchel into Thomas's midriff, nearly knocking him down.

Thomas hefted the heavy satchel. "Hardly seems a fair trade."

"Take them to the library for a quick look and see what you can make of them before luncheon, while I go change." He had mastered the second flight of stairs and was seeing spots before his eyes when Roslyn left her room and gave him a concerned look.

"You are deathly pale. Has anything happened?"

He staggered a little and she caught him with her shoulder under his armpit. "There is blood on your back. Where is your room?" she asked.

"The end of the hall."

She helped him there. He turned the knob, and she

kicked the door open, then sat him on the bed.

"You've been stabbed."

"More like sliced."

"I'm going for help."

"If you do, the servants will talk of it and frighten Caroline."

"What can I do?"

"Help me off with this coat."

She peeled the offending garment off, then tore the already ruined shirt to expose a three-inch wound. "This needs stitches. We must call a surgeon."

"Can you stitch it? I know it's a lot to ask."

"Your valet should be doing this, or a surgeon."

"My last valet would not lift a finger to save me if I were bleeding to death. I am glad he sacked himself."

"You should hire another, one who would not mind rips in you or your clothes."

"Please, Roslyn. Your sister would be upset."

She seemed on the point of refusing but finally gave a thin smile. "I will get my sewing kit."

While she was gone Mark reached for the brandy bottle and took a deep drink.

She took it from him when she came back and spilled a little into a glass to soak her thread and needle.

He stared at her in surprise. "You've done this before."

"I did stitch Tess's knee when she split it open. Her father did not think she was worth the price of a doctor visit. Now hold still." She poured water in a basin and bathed the area.

"That sounds like Luther."

"You are not going to groan or wince, are you?"

"I hope not. I can barely feel your needle."

"Injury has a natural numbing effect."

Mark wondered if that was why Roslyn seemed so often distant and aloof. Had she been injured beyond repair?

When she was done, she applied a bandage, then helped him into a fresh shirt and coat.

"I still think we should tell someone."

"Vincent knows."

"What—what do you mean?"

"I found him at the townhouse this morning. He was as shocked as a jaded soldier could be that I was attacked on my way there."

Roslyn gave a sigh of relief. "I worried what had become of him. He wrote that he had made no headway with the solicitor, but he did not say where he was."

"I have asked him to be a joint guardian to the children."

"I wish you had not done that."

"Surely you trust your own brother?"

"I do not know Vincent anymore, not since he came back from the war. He is always so somber and we hardly speak. I think there is something broken in him that can never be mended. I'm not sure he can handle such a task. Would it push him over the edge?"

"I thought it prudent to recruit him as an ally, and I believe he needs such a burden. It will give him purpose and occupation now that there is no war."

"That does not make him—Oh, I see. In case you would be killed."

"You are quick. Also, he was eating breakfast while I was being attacked and was nearly three-quarters of the way through the *Times*. He could not possibly have done it."

Roslyn lifted her fine gray gaze to him in amazement, though he did not know what puzzled her: was it his clear thinking, or his audacity?

Finally she said, "Nor would he know you planned to go there or what route you would take. But someone knew."

"Someone in the house? No, perhaps I was being watched. I took much the same route as I would use to go to the bank."

"I would rather think that than have a spy within, but we have to consider both possibilities."

"You have a naturally suspicious mind." He said it in an admiring way as though he had complimented her hair.

She nodded her acceptance of this assessment as she packed up her kit. "It has kept us alive."

"Were there other threats?"

"Only from Raby."

"What a life you have led. I wish I could say such threats are over, but we must still be cautious."

"More so after today. What shall we do with these bloody rags?"

"Wad them up and stuff them in my briefcase. I shall ditch them in the river."

When they reached the luncheon parlor, Tess asked, "Are you sure we cannot go today?"

"I have been away a bit and must catch up on paperwork today. Besides, there will not be any sales until tomorrow. Meason, will you see if Thomas can join us for lunch?"

Thomas came in a few minutes later. "I have only made a start."

"It will wait," Mark said.

Elizabeth introduced Thomas to Caroline, Roslyn, and Tess.

"I have met Tess. She has been helping me in the library."

"How?" Caroline asked.

"With the expense accounts."

Tess looked up at her mother. "We did not get any beeswax candles, Mother, did we?"

"Not for years and years."

"Then I was right."

Mark looked up from the trout on his plate. "I take it Mr. Hardwick recorded some questionable expenses?"

Thomas blew out a tired breath. "I think they are all questionable, but more on that later."

"Is there any use?" Caroline asked. "We can never recover any of that money."

Mark shook his head. "Probably not, though I need to know the depth of his crimes for my suit against him. But let us think lighter thoughts today. What shall we do this afternoon? It is not cold or rainy. We could drive about London, shop and see the sights."

Caroline laughed. "*I* have been here before. You all go touring, but I would prefer to enjoy your excellent library. Tess can't stop talking about it. And I may even be of some help to Mr. Winslow in his examination of the accounts."

Elizabeth smiled. "I shall stay home with Caroline and Thomas. You three go and have fun."

"I will have them hitch up the curricle."

Roslyn's eyes bulged a little. "Perhaps an enclosed carriage with a driver, in case we have packages."

Mark winced and moved his arm experimentally. Driving might tug the wound open. "Yes, of course.

What was I thinking?"

A driving tour of the parks preceded a jaunt down Oxford Street with stops at three shops. Most of the ribbons and figured muslin they bought were for Tess. Roslyn dismissed any attempt to pull out bolts of silk or sarsenet for her or Caroline.

They were just getting into the carriage with the last packages when Tess found a grubby tabby kitten huddling in the crack between two buildings. She scooped it up immediately.

Roslyn sighed. "Oh, Tess."

"It is just so hungry. Please, Mark?"

"Of course we could use a cat. It can stay in your room. We will get the stable lads to bring up a box of sand."

Tess cuddled the animal up in a corner of the lap robe, and it seemed to fall asleep. Tess looked soon to follow it.

Mark whispered to Roslyn, "I must remember not to wear her out like this."

"That is *not* why I sent you that condemning look. You have just set a dangerous precedent."

"It might be possible to overdo compassion, but it is an impulse I would never discourage in her."

"When he was a boy, Vincent used to bring home every stray dog he found."

"I see. Being hungry and wanting for care himself, his impulse was to share."

"We had little enough to eat, but he managed to hunt enough to feed his pack in the stable. It was brutal of Father to send him into the army."

"Was Vincent the only son? Why did he have to go?"

"To disguise the fact that the estate was beggared

and would have to be sold. Caroline and I were glad to escape."

"What happened to your parents?"

"They moved to Bath. The letters stopped, as you know, and I had no funds to visit them. I will write again to the last address, but it has been years. If they are still alive, we would surely have heard something."

"You would never have left Caroline anyway. So Vincent had no home, then."

"I suppose when he came back it was natural to find us, then hang on Luther either at Glassmere or the townhouse." She bit her lip at how badly her brother had been treated by her father. What right had she to condemn old Lord Cahill or Luther since her own father had done far worse?

"But as a protector," Mark reminded her.

Roslyn thought for a moment. "I always hoped he would defend us if it became necessary."

Mark lowered his voice, though the coachman could not have heard them over the noise of traffic. "He says Raby is a real threat to you."

She thought about the sneering lord and felt so safe now from his lascivious looks it was easy to answer Mark. "I can handle Raby."

"I am happy to know it. At any rate, I have asked your brother to call, and also to reside at the townhouse to protect it."

She found herself smiling at his presumption. "Another snap decision on your part?"

"I am better at those than at logic or asking permission. Thomas is always on me about my impulses, but usually all turns out well."

"Let us hope your mother feels the same about the

cat as you do."

"Oh, Geoff, drive past the warehouse on our way home. I want to show Roslyn the quay."

The driver crossed London Bridge and guided the team east along the south bank, which surprised Roslyn. She had thought the docks were all on the north bank.

"This is St. Savior's Dock."

"How appropriate." She looked at the small dock reaching out into the muddy Thames and at the neat brick warehouse.

Mark smiled at her. "We use smaller boats to move cargo off the ships or on, since the biggest of them would ground out when heavily laden. But it is near the warehouse."

"How many ships do you have?"

"Three for now. Business can expand unexpectedly, especially when you make snap decisions. The warehouse is brick, four stories, and relatively fireproof."

"Those big double doors?"

"One set on each of the upper floors. We winch cargo in and out of them. Saves much time."

"The building is huge."

"Another time, when Tess is awake, we will go inside, and on one of the ships."

Shortly after, they arrived back at the house and heard laughter coming from the library.

Thomas was calling out items to Caroline and she was responding in the negative as though it was a game. When they walked in, his mother looked up with a sparkle in her eyes.

"Hardwick was such a dolt," she said. "No one could run through that much salt even if it had been purchased."

Mark shook his head. "So glad we have a sense of humor about the extortion. I am sure a judge will see it differently."

Roslyn took Tess and the kitten upstairs since they both needed a bath. Mark called Thomas into the hall to ask him to bring some silks from the warehouse the next day.

"I will hunt them out myself. Did you sign those contracts?"

"They must still be in my bedroom."

"I shall fetch them."

Mark waited in the hallway, wondering if he should tell Thomas about the attack. When Thomas came back down, he had the contracts in one hand and Mark's briefcase in the other.

"Why did you not say you were wounded?"

"Trying not to upset the ladies. Could you ditch that satchel of gore in the Thames for me?"

"That is one of the stranger tasks you have assigned me. Are you sure you are going to be all right?"

"I am fine. More blood than anything. Please come into the library and I will sign those."

Mark was just finishing when Vincent was announced. "You may as well come into the library, Captain Clary. We all seem to prefer it as a place to gather," Mark said from behind the big desk. "By the way, this is Thomas Winslow, the man who keeps the business running smoothly."

Vincent hesitated on the threshold of the room, then came and greeted Thomas. That gave Caroline time to rise. Mark saw tears in her eyes as she rushed into her brother's arms.

"I was worried about you," she said when she released him.

Mark could hear Vincent's sigh of relief. "I would have rescued you if I could."

"I know that. Please sit."

The elder Lady Cahill smiled. "I have sent for tea, but there is brandy on the table if you gentlemen would like something stronger."

Vincent went to take her hand. "So we have two dowager Lady Cahills now."

"Yes, news of my death was premature."

Mark went to pour three brandies, gave one to Thomas, and when he handed one to the ex-soldier whispered, "Don't say anything about the attack."

"Of course not." Vincent gave a slight bow.

Roslyn entered then and hesitated, but her reaction was much like Caroline's only without the tears. When she released her brother she said, "We are all safe now."

"Yes, your knight in shining armor seems to have done the trick."

Mark laughed. "More like tarnished armor. If I had any brains, I would have thought of a solution long ago."

Vincent looked up at him, the creases on his face relaxing into a smile. "How did the tour go?"

"Found lots of fabric and ribbon for Tess," Mark said.

"And she has adopted a kitten," Roslyn added.

Caroline gasped. "Oh, no."

Elizabeth laughed. "I am sure we can always use another cat. We have only the old gray one in the kitchen, and she seems disinclined to mouse anywhere else."

"Mark has also promised Tess a horse," Roslyn said to her brother.

Mark noted Vincent's raised brow. "If we can find a safe one. Would you like to come with us to Tattersalls tomorrow?"

"I would be happy to."

They prevailed on Vincent to stay for dinner. Since it was to be a family dinner, he agreed. Tess smiled at him and he asked if she had a riding dress yet.

"We bought fabric, but it won't be finished by tomorrow. Maybe she can wear a work skirt for now," Roslyn said.

"You mean I might be riding as early as tomorrow?"

Mark smiled. "We have at least two sidesaddles, but we will go in the carriage tomorrow."

The siblings did not reminisce about the past the way most brothers and sisters would. Mark could only conclude that they had not many good memories of it. He could believe that, since he had few himself. He had to contrive to make the future not quite so desperate for them. Odd how even just meeting them he felt a bond, an empathy for their troubles now that his own had been solved. When one has been fortunate enough to make a comfortable place for himself in the world, it only made sense to want to share the bounty.

And this was family, after all, a thing his mother had been deprived of. Though he would rather consider Roslyn as someone he might marry, it was early days to be thinking of that. He could see obstacles in his way, not the least of which was her vow not to marry. He had a way of getting around people by just making things happen, then asking forgiveness for any blunders, but somehow he thought Roslyn would see through that strategy.

Chapter Five

After breakfast, Roslyn put the finishing touches on a makeshift riding dress for Tess. She changed into her own riding habit, then went to find the girl. She stopped when she heard from the morning room exclamations of delight. Roslyn entered to find happy faces and a blaze of colors. A sheaf of silk draped on the sofa was of such a soft blue it could almost be called snow. An emerald green bolt caught her eye and she went to feel it. Thomas brought her a bolt of pale pink cloth. "This would become you as well. There is also the amber."

"But where did they come from?" she asked.

"The warehouse," Thomas said. "Some fabric never sells, so we store it hoping for an order later."

Somehow Roslyn doubted these had even been offered for sale, but she would never say such a thing. Thomas was smiling too brightly at Caroline's plans for dresses.

The older Lady Cahill looked benignly on the excited mother and child. "My dressmaker will be here before lunch. Then you have a physician to interview this afternoon."

Tess jumped up from the floor. "I forgot. My horse! We may be late already."

"Here is your temporary riding dress, just in case. Run and put it on." Roslyn found herself smiling as well. She could not remember being this happy at any time in recent history.

When Tess and Roslyn got to the courtyard, Vincent and Mark were already there. Besides the coachman to drive the team, a groom hopped up behind, Roslyn assumed to lead whatever they bought. That way Mark would not tear open his wound. So he could be prudent when much depended on it. Still, she did not think he would be more careful in future.

Something else was bothering her. She already felt too beholden to Mark for all his gifts and kindnesses. But this pony was for Tess, and he had promised. The drive to the horse auction took no more than half an hour. Before the sale they were permitted to walk along the rows of stalls and look at the horses. Tess ran from one to another, petting each horse. Roslyn did not see anything suitable for a child.

She stroked the nose of a lithe gray mare she could have fallen in love with, but she looked too energetic for Tess.

"I think we are looking in the wrong place for a small grade horse," Vincent said. "Let us try the market."

Mark glanced at him. "I never thought of that."

Before Mark got back into the carriage, he had a conference with his groom, gave him something, and then left the man at the sale. Coventry market was to the west of the city and was more farm animals and cabbages than horses, but there were a few ponies for sale and one small bay mare. The horse was not young, but when Tess ran up and kissed her on the nose she whickered at her.

Mark was about to approach the owner, but Vincent said, "Let me," and hustled them off to look at lambs, baby goats, ducks and geese, each of which Tess would have adored to have if Roslyn had not forbidden it. Tess would have to wait for their return to the estate to acquire any more livestock. When they turned to go back to the carriage, Vincent was leading the mare.

"Uncle Vincent! You bought her for me!" Tess hugged him about the waist, and he smiled down on her. "She can only carry a light load but will be fine for you. Her name is Bonny."

"It is a long way back to the house," Roslyn said.

"I can lead her," Vincent claimed.

Roslyn smiled. "I was going to suggest I saddle her and walk her beside the carriage so Tess can study her conformation."

"Good idea," Mark voted.

"When can I ride her?" Tess asked.

"She may be tired from her journey from the country," her uncle said. "Let us see how she is in the morning."

They took their time driving back from the market and even stopped for street food for Tess. Roslyn thought the mare was calm enough for an excitable child yet able to endure a long ride. When they got back to the stables, there was also the gray mare she had looked at for herself. So that was why the groom had stayed at the horse market, she perceived.

While Vincent and Tess fed and watered Bonny, Roslyn caressed the face of the new mare. Mark came and stood behind her.

"It is too much," she whispered, fighting to hold back tears.

He put a gentle hand on the mare's neck. "I had to rescue her. Did you see the great toad who was looking at her? He would have broken her back or wind."

Roslyn sniffed. "Oh, so you brought her to rescue

her, not to please me?"

He thought for a moment. "I'm sure you are pleased she is safe."

"You are impossible."

"Thank you. We are terribly late for dinner, and certainly for changing for dinner."

"I can be ready in five minutes."

"A challenge. It takes me that long to tie a fresh neck cloth."

Worn out from the day's adventure, Tess did not join them at dinner, but Thomas did.

"Not to mix work with home life, but do you have a report for me?" Mark asked.

"I estimate Hardwick has robbed the estate of close to eight thousand pounds since your father died. Before then the books seem fairly clean."

"That is odd. I would have thought Luther kept better control of things than Father."

Elizabeth cleared her throat. "Before you both rescued me, I did the accounts at Glassmere. I should not have abandoned my position."

Mark looked at his mother. "You are entitled to a life."

No more was said, but what Mark thought and would not bring up at dinner was that Hardwick might have had a motive for killing both Luther and his father. The thought that followed close on the heels of the first was that they were better off without his father and brother and eight thousand pounds was a cheap price to be rid of them.

He glanced round the table wondering if anyone else was having such ungenerous thoughts. Caroline seemed interested only in the dishes set before her—the chicken, rice, and spring peas. But Roslyn had a crease between her pretty eyebrows.

When she caught up with him in the library later, she asked to see the list.

"The list of losses?"

"No, the list of suspects, of course."

Mark pulled it from the desk drawer and presented her with a pen and inkwell. "Striking out or adding?"

"I just wanted to make sure Lord Raby was on here."

"What have you thought of?"

"Something he said to me the night of Luther's death. It only just came to me."

"What?"

She hesitated so long Mark's amused look turned to one of dread.

"Only that he would have me then or in a day's time, so there was no point in me evading him."

"A day's time. And how did you evade him?"

"I seared the back of his hand with a candle."

Mark chuckled. "Effective."

"One uses the weapons one has at hand."

"What happened then? Please sit down."

"I secreted Tess in the maid's room and Caroline in mine. When Luther demanded his wife, I said she was praying for his soul."

"He believed that?"

"He wasn't just drunk at that point so much as deranged."

"Could he have been poisoned and the doctor missed it?"

"He complained of his stomach for months before that. I should have told them that at the inquest, but I did not want them to think we did him in."

"No one would think that."

"If you saw the way he ate, you would understand why his stomach hurt. There may have been no connection."

Mark walked to the fireplace and kicked at one log. "I thought the magistrate and doctor were just being self-important."

"If not for the attack on you, I would have assumed the same." She looked at him, trying to figure out what was going through his mind.

"Yes, and that happened after Vincent had the books. The embezzlement would have come out if Luther was dead or not."

"Perhaps revenge?"

"That wasn't old Hardwick on the horse, so unless he would give up a stash of his ill-gotten money to hire an assassin, it must be someone else. Besides, I got a threatening letter from him. He means to sue me for breach of contract."

"Can he do that?" Roslyn asked.

"I doubt he had a contract. Most agents work at will. Still he would not try to kill me before I reply, would he?"

Roslyn froze as she thought through all he had said. "So there is something else, something worse that you may find out. And that someone has to silence you for."

Mark raised an eyebrow at her perception of the problem. "I wish I knew what it was."

"And who wants you dead," she reminded him.

"We still do not know if Caroline is in danger."

There was a knock and Thomas came in, trailed by Vincent.

"The other ladies have gone to bed," Thomas said.

"With visions of evening gowns dancing in their heads." Roslyn smiled. "I will leave you gentlemen to your brandy and cigars."

Mark touched her arm. "Stay a minute. Thomas, can you help me trace our relations to see who the next heir is after me? We will have to get Mother to help us with that."

Thomas sighed. "Sounds like immense fun."

"More like a dead bore, but your sarcasm is appreciated."

Vincent looked at Roslyn. "Shall I do the same for our few relatives? We have a maiden aunt in Spittlefields who might be able to fill us in, though I doubt our side can be the murderous lot. No motive."

Mark shrugged. "I doubt it too, but take your aunt a basket of victuals for her trouble."

"If that is all, I have sewing to do before we ride tomorrow."

Roslyn mounted the stairs, enjoying the low rumble of voices from the library. Yes, she liked being included in their short council of war, but she liked better that Vincent was getting along with Mark and Thomas. He needed companionship and occupation. Perhaps Mark was right that Vincent needed to feel necessary to their welfare. Most importantly, her brother needed to feel powerful again. She could understand that, for it was the same thing she needed.

Chapter Six

It was sunny the next day, and Tess proudly appeared in her new blue riding dress at breakfast. Vincent came in time to share breakfast with them. They decided to ride only in the closer parks on the south side of the river.

"I will shepherd Tess with my old war horse, who barely plods. If you two want to exercise your mounts, you can circle back to us."

They opted to keep pace with Tess and Vincent for this first ride. The child listened to Vincent and went no faster than a trot on her mare.

"I am so happy Vincent has taken an interest in Tess."

Mark smiled at her. "I am as well. A man needs family by him or nothing seems worthwhile."

"You should know, driven from your home."

"To tell you the truth, I was glad to get away. It was not so bad when I was at school, but the holidays were torture."

Roslyn studied her mare for a moment. "I was glad to escape my home as well."

"We have much in common then."

"Is that why you are so good to us?"

He smiled. "It makes me feel good."

"You cannot keep buying us gifts."

"But I get joy from that. I have no siblings. Mother

63

does not need anything."

"I see. I am like a sister to you?" Roslyn teased.

"Caroline is my sister-in-law. You are something else entirely."

"I do not even ask what that is."

He tilted the brim of his hat at her. "Intellectually a worthy opponent and ally."

"And physically?" Roslyn could hardly believe she had asked that.

"A damned attractive woman—sorry, that slipped out, but you are."

"I told you I will never marry."

"But that does not mean you should not have some fun. I have a box at the theater I hardly use. If Mother has the energy, we should go tonight. Perhaps Vincent will accompany us."

"Why not Thomas?"

"He actually uses the box more than I do, but I sense he would rather stand guard at home over Caroline and Tess."

"Stand guard? I thought you were throwing them together in a spate of matchmaking?"

"That may happen on its own." Mark smiled. "Would you be upset if they made a match of it? Thomas will soon be made a partner."

"On the contrary, he makes my sister laugh and is good with Tess. It would be the best possible outcome. But are you making him a partner in case you should be murdered?"

Mark laughed. "No, because he deserves it, though things will be smoother with him in charge if anything does happen."

Roslyn felt her lips tremble. He did run on swords.

"Do you think they need a guard at your home?"

"I'm not sure of anything except that we will have to hire more help if I keep stealing Thomas away from the shipping office."

"We should not be your burden or his."

Tess turned and waved at them. Mark waved back. "Not a burden, but a delightful distraction. Better to be all together here than some of us riding back and forth to Glassmere to check on you."

"Unless we catch the murderer by the end of the season."

"I know, or it will not be safe to send you back there. Perhaps you can stay."

Roslyn tilted her head. "Or move to the town house."

"Oh, it needs work. Too many years of neglect, and there is no staff. But that is an option if we do not smoke out the culprit."

"With you as bait?"

"Better me than an innocent babe."

"What makes you so sure it will be a boy?"

"I do not know, but that reminds me we have a closer deadline than the end of the season. We need to find the murderer before the baby comes."

She rode in silence for a moment before she stared at him. "When you think about it, there is no point at all in killing you yet."

"What?"

"Your death will only be necessary if the baby is a girl."

Mark coughed. "You do think of the damnedest things. So that should set my mind at rest?"

"No silly. It should set you to thinking. If not

because you are temporarily Lord Cahill, why is someone trying to kill you?".

"I wish you were not so much smarter than me. No, I do not mean that. I should be glad you think of these things before I do. It gives me an edge."

\*\*\*\*

Lunch that day was a raucous affair with Tess describing how well her horse had done and Vincent complimenting her riding. Tess also planned to acquire a plethora of livestock at the market before they returned to Glassmere.

Caroline sighed and rested her cheek on her hand. "I think it was easier to manage when we were poor."

Roslyn smiled. They were still poor, just riding the coattails of a benefactor. If she had not loved the mare so much, she would have rejected it. That would have been terribly ungracious, but she did not want to be forever beholden to Mark, no matter how much she liked him. Did her feelings go beyond liking? She admired him, and she would dearly miss him if she were never to see him again, but she would survive as she had survived all the other reverses in her life. Still, why push him away for the sake of pride?

Vincent finally cleared his throat. "I journey to Spittlefields this afternoon to seek out Aunt Sadie. I should take a notebook and pencil in case she does recall something."

"Would you like me to come with you?" Roslyn asked. "She might remember me."

"She might be more inclined to let me in if you are there to lend me credit."

Thomas jumped up. "I too should discuss the family tree with you, Lady Cahill, and see if we can discover a likely murderer."

Elizabeth smiled sadly and with a hint of worry on her brow. "You know, I should be upset that murder is why we are discussing the family, but it just makes it more exciting."

Mark pushed himself back from the table. "I think I will give that a pass, since I am far behind with work. Of course, that means a trip to the office."

Thomas blinked. "I left all the contracts and important correspondence in the library."

"How convenient. I should get to it."

The trip to Spittlefields turned out to be a fool's errand. They had started inquiring at churches, then moved on to shopkeepers, but no one in living memory had heard of Sadie Clary. Vincent brought Roslyn back to the house, then went to the town house to change for the theater.

While Caroline rested upstairs, Roslyn sewed quietly in the drawing room. There was a cozy fire and the comforting sound of Thomas and Lady Cahill discussing relatives while they looked at a chart in the family Bible. Also, some volumes on the peerage were open on the low table.

A footman announcing Lord Raby made her wish they had said they were not at home to callers. She had a moment's notion to flee, but that would leave Lady Cahill and Thomas to fend him off when they had no idea how dangerous he was.

He bowed and greeted Lady Cahill, then seemed to dismiss Thomas—or try to.

Roslyn put her sewing aside to greet him and introduce Thomas so that he would not abandon them. Besides, Mark was in the next room in case they needed him. "How did you know we were in town?"

Raby gave a slight bow. "Rumor had it you were staying here."

"Really. Who told you?"

"I don't recall, but I thought I should see how you go on."

Roslyn looked up at him. "Quite well."

"May I have a moment alone?"

"Certainly not. That would be highly improper."

Thomas stood, and Lady Cahill cleared her throat.

"Any more thoughts on our relationship?" Raby asked.

"We have no relationship. My only thought is that I would like to never see you again."

Thomas was looking alarmed now, his brown hair drifting across his forehead.

"You will run into me everywhere." Raby gave a sweeping gesture.

"In fact, you are on our list, the top of our list," Roslyn continued.

"List of what? Eligible suitors?"

"Suspects in Luther's murder," she replied.

Thomas snorted a laugh.

"The magistrate is insane. I had no reason to kill my friend."

Roslyn glanced at her hostess, who also seemed on the point of giggles. "If he had really been your friend, you would not have fleeced him."

"You know nothing about it."

Mark had almost finished the contracts when he heard raised voices next door and one of them from Roslyn. He went to see what the problem was.

"Raby? You here? Why, I left word you were not to

be admitted."

"A courtesy call."

"You seem to be distressing my mother and Miss Clary. That does not smack of courtesy."

"I would like to speak to you privately."

"By all means. Come with me."

"Where are we going?" Raby asked as he followed Mark into the hall.

"To the door."

"You cannot get rid of me. Luther owes me close to five thousand pounds. I have the vowels right here." He patted his pocket.

"Do not bother to get your IOUs out. Even if I believed that was my brother's signature, even if I thought your card games had not taken advantage of a drunk, even if the estate had the money, I would not pay them."

"They are debts of honor," Raby claimed.

"There is nothing honorable about fleecing an incompetent, knowing you are beggaring his wife and child."

"There is an alternative." Raby's snakelike gaze darted to the closed door of the drawing room.

"I will give you an alternative. Leave under your own power, or I shall have you thrown out."

"Cahill promised me Roslyn to forgive the debts."

Mark felt his jaw clench and his heart thud in his chest just before he exploded and backed Raby up against the wall with his left hand around his throat. "So my brother was into human trafficking as well? If I reported such a demand to the local magistrate, you would have broken some very important laws, namely the prohibition against slavery! What do you have to say to that?"

"Probably nothing unless you stop strangling him," Thomas said.

Mark glanced over his shoulder at Thomas and eased his hold.

"Women are bought and sold all the time," Raby squeaked. "We just put a better name on it—marriage."

Mark exhaled and felt as though he was breathing fire. "You impose on Miss Clary again and I will dispense with the magistrate. I will kill you myself and dump your corpse in the Thames where you belong. Meason, show him out or throw him out and never admit him again. Please tell all the new staff."

"Very good, my lord."

Roslyn was also in the hall but waited for Raby's exit before she commented, "He could have called you out for at least three of the things you said."

"You heard? I know, that is what I was hoping." Mark straightened his cuffs, then winced and shrugged his bad shoulder.

"Hoping?" Roslyn asked. "He is accounted an excellent shot. If you are courting death at his hands, then a stray assassin or two won't even matter."

Mark tamed his anger, and when he turned, his gaze swept over the hall clock. "God, look at the time. Better dress if we are going to the theater tonight."

"After what just happened? He will gossip about us to everyone."

"All the more reason to make an appearance."

Lady Cahill came out. "Mark is right. We must put in an appearance tonight."

When they went up the stairs, Mark turned to Thomas. "I know how you love the theater."

Thomas smiled. "But if Caroline does not go, it would be as well I stayed home to guard her."

"Thank you. Quite a time saver, you having a room here instead of a place of your own."

"For you, anyway."

"Are you ill-used?"

"No, for everything is exciting, even you getting stabbed."

"Stay alert. You look too much like me for comfort. Someone could mistake us."

Thomas waggled his eyebrows. "That is what I mean by exciting."

****

Elizabeth glanced around the softly lit Agora theater. "There is hardly anyone here tonight."

"Last week for this play," Vincent said as he waved to some army friends in the pit.

Lady Cahill tapped her fan on her other hand in a measured way. "I know what we should do—throw an evening soiree, not a tea for ladies but a quiet entertainment for couples. Punch and cakes. There will be music and all my dearest friends."

Lady Cahill had lent Roslyn an ivory silk gown and fur pelisse for the night, and also a pearl necklace. She felt beholden again, though she did enjoy wearing such lovely things. "Do you want me to play the piano for your entertainment?" Roslyn asked.

"Could you? Just a few pieces? My old fingers are too stiff. Thomas can play. Not Mark."

Mark leaned forward in his chair to make eye contact with Vincent. "I am a sad disappointment to her. Thomas actually studied music, but there are few positions available for musicians if you don't know anyone."

Roslyn smiled at him. "I am glad he found you."

"He was my school mate. A scholarship student. Took a first in maths. Come to think of it, he is smarter than me in other subjects as well."

Vincent cast a dubious gaze at Mark. "I am sure he cannot excel you in modesty. What did you study?"

"History, Latin, and theology."

The Clarys both stared at Mark in amazement.

"There was some notion of turning me into a cleric." Mark said this with a twist to his smile that emphasized the silliness of it.

Roslyn choked down a laugh, and Vincent leaned back with a satisfied smile.

Lady Cahill fanned herself. "We could not think what else to do with him."

"There was always the army or the navy," Mark said.

"I consider I saved your life by not letting you go," his mother said. "You were always running on arrows, in the ordinary way of things."

Roslyn knew the expression was *falling on a sword*. She saw Vincent open his mouth to correct Lady Cahill, but he closed it again with a smile.

"She means I was accident prone."

"Not like *now*," Vincent said.

Mark shook his head.

Roslyn almost said it was no accident that slashed his shoulder, but she did not know if he had told his mother about the incident, since they had kept it from Caroline.

Many people acknowledged Lady Cahill with a smile and nod. They came to chat with her during the intermission. She invited them all to her soiree. The one she had just thought of. How wonderful to be able to plan an event and just do it without worrying over the cost.

On the way home Roslyn tried to decide on the pieces she would practice. She had been in the music room and admired the grand piano but was still feeling too stressed to play. Now she had a task and only a few days to regain her skill. Perhaps Thomas would alternate with her.

They dropped Vincent at the town house. Mark asked him to accompany him to the solicitor's office in the morning.

"If you think we can make any headway, I shall meet you there when they open."

When they got out of the carriage at home, Roslyn watched as Mark helped his mother across the stable yard and in the back door. She followed them and smiled as he led his mother up the stairs. He came back down, meeting her in the hall where she tarried for no good reason.

"I was considering checking on Tess and Caroline."

"You do not want to wake them. You were planning the music?"

"How did you know?"

He smiled. "You were humming a bit."

"How annoying of me."

"Not really. It was sweet of you to offer to play at the soiree."

"It is something I can do to repay all the kindness your mother has shown. I cannot think of any way to repay *you*."

He almost shrugged but stopped before he pinched his wound. "Being of use is my payment. There were a good many years when I was not much use to anyone."

Roslyn knew the feeling. "So you look for impossible deeds to perform?"

"Let us say I do not miss an opportunity."

She nodded, then looked up the stairs.

"You are wondering if Caroline and the child will ever be safe," Mark said.

"Is thought reading one of your skills? Yes, if we do not figure out who killed Luther, neither Tess nor the baby will ever be safe. I almost hope it is a girl, but that would put *you* in even more danger."

"I do not want to be Lord Cahill. Twenty years or so will be enough time for people to forget how much they hate the name. Caroline's little boy by then will inherit an estate that is no longer impoverished."

"And what will you be doing in those years besides looking over your shoulder for an assassin?"

"Trying to make things right. Helping with the children, possibly marrying you."

She turned her head away, and he raised his left hand and turned her face back toward him.

"I thought you were going to say Caroline."

"There is a very good law against taking a widowed sister-in-law to wife. Besides, you are the one I have fallen in love with."

She gave an impatient toss of her head. "That is too bad."

"Oh, well, it was worth a shot." He moved toward the library.

"I only meant that we are in no state to be thinking of ourselves."

"So true. We must make all safe first."

"Are you not going to bed?"

"If I know Thomas, he is waiting in the library with mail or paperwork. Possibly even a contract."

"Poor Thomas. When does he ever get to sleep?"

"Almost never. We figured out long ago it's easier for him to live here. We are no more than twenty minutes from the dock and warehouse. Makes it so much faster to communicate."

"And for you to work him twenty hours a day instead of ten."

"Do you think I overwork him?"

"I think he would not complain if you did. Now that he is tasked with guarding Caroline, he has no life."

Mark came back a few steps. "Considering the attraction there, which grows stronger by the day, I do not think he regards his time with Caroline as work."

"Nothing should happen between them for ten months."

"While Caroline pretends to mourn a horrible husband?"

"Put like that, it does not make any sense to wait. But nothing can happen anyway until we find the murderer."

"That will give Thomas a greater incentive to help us. If we find the assassin, that frees up you as well."

She studied his face, searching for meaning or another joke. "To do what?"

"Make a life of your own."

"With you?"

"It is a possibility, though not the only one. To be frank, there were quite a few other men trying to catch your attention tonight."

"Why? I am not an heiress."

"But you carry yourself as though you are, as well

as if in complete control of any situation."

"I have had to act that part to keep us safe."

"I should not remind you, then."

"That my poise is all that is standing between me and utter ruin?" She was almost in tears and could not stop herself leaning into him when he embraced her.

"Things will get better and better. Someday you will not even think of those desperate years. They are behind you now."

She pushed herself back from him. "Not yet. We all still live on a knife's edge. That I cannot forget." She used both hands to dash the tears from her eyes and went up the stairs as though she were the Queen. If this skill was all she had, she should not lose her knack for it.

Chapter Seven

Vincent was waiting for him on Fleet Street outside the office of Hastings and Whitcomb. When Mark hopped out of the hackney, Vincent folded his newspaper, tucked it under his arm, and opened the street door. The offices were up a flight of dusty stairs.

A pernicious-looking clerk rose from his stool when they arrived. "Mr. Hastings cannot see you today."

"I have an appointment," Mark said.

"Something urgent came up."

"Very well. Inform him that the Cahill estate business, including probating the will, is being transferred to my solicitor, who does have time to see me."

"Wait! You cannot do this. We are in possession of the will." The clerk clutched a fat folder to his chest.

"So there is a will," Mark said. "And you will be asked to produce that in court."

"There are certain fees."

"Which will go to my solicitor now," Mark countered.

"But we have always handled the Cahill estate."

Vincent glared at the clerk. "More like mishandled it."

"You cannot get anywhere without the will."

"I don't believe you have it," Vincent said.

"I need not show it to you." The clerk closed up the

folder and pushed it into the shelf behind him.

Mark blew out an impatient breath. "We cannot await your whim. There is a child who needs a guardian. And I think you are lying about Hastings not being in. I will see for myself."

"No, do not go in there!" The clerk jumped to throw his thin body in Mark's way, with the effect of Mark opening the door and pushing the clerk inside with him.

"Who do you think you are?" the clerk demanded.

"He is Lord Cahill," Vincent said as he tweaked a beribboned document out of the folder and cracked it open.

The astonished clerk struggled to get out of Mark's grasp and grabbed for the document, but too late. Vincent slapped his hand aside as he scanned it.

"This is rich. Luther's only bequest is ten thousand pounds to Hardwick, who is named custodian of the estate and guardian of Tess."

"Even Luther would never be so stupid." Mark held the clerk by the coat collar as he looked at the parchment Vincent held out. "And that is not his handwriting or his signature."

Vincent held the paper to the light. "That is not my signature below it, either, and I was supposed to have witnessed this document. This is a forgery that Hardwick gave you. If there is a real will, he destroyed it or hid it."

"This is a replacement for the old will, and it was given to me by Mr. Hardwick."

"Are you aware he is a suspect in a murder investigation?" Mark asked. "Luther St. John's murder?"

The clerk's teeth were chattering. "Nothing has been proven."

"This was authored by Hardwick," Vincent accused.

"If this were ever executed, Tess would be murdered. Probably Caroline as well. The question remains, is this firm a party to this forgery or just another victim?"

"I know nothing about it. Give that back."

"No, we carry it to my solicitor, who will assume your duties."

"We have not been paid."

"You have not done anything," Mark stated. "I will tell you we have brought an action against Hardwick for embezzlement. He has beggared the estate. I can easily amend that to include the firm of Hasting and Whitcomb, if you really want to stay in this dog fight."

When the clerk was reduced to babbling, they left, taking the fake will with them.

Mark hailed a hackney, which is to say he stepped out in front of one and grabbed the horse's reins.

"Here now," the driver complained. "You might have been kilt."

Vincent shook his head and got in beside Mark.

"Hardwick is a complete villain. I shall prosecute him to the fullest extent."

"Why don't I just kill him?" Vincent asked. "It would save time."

"That would be too merciful. I want him to suffer."

"As you wish. Where to now?"

"My solicitor's office."

"So you expected we would not get satisfaction from this firm."

"Since *you* have been unable to budge them, I was sure we would not. If only we had the original will, that would help."

"Are you sure about that?"

"No."

\*\*\*\*

Mark and Vincent returned from their day's work with satisfied smiles, so Roslyn assumed they had been successful. Vincent joined them for dinner. She also suspected he was preparing London to meet them, for he had added several couples to Lady Clary's list of guests for the soiree.

The meal was another revelation to her: salmon and some exotic rice, fresh butter beans, and tasty scallops in a sauce. Then a roulade of beef she was almost too full to sample. So she did not prod the men for news. That would be the dessert.

Finally, as the fruit and nut dishes were passed around, she looked an inquiry at Vincent.

"Yes we have made some progress toward getting Tess and the baby protected."

"Our solicitor will attempt to get orphan's court to approve Caroline and Roslyn as guardians of the children and Vincent and me as executors of the estate. Of course, that will wait until the baby comes, so we have a name."

Roslyn nodded. "I see. Spreading our cards."

"What do you mean?" Caroline asked.

"The more of us involved, the less risk," Vincent replied.

She nodded. "Of course, in case one of us should be killed." She wrapped her arms around her stomach protectively.

Mark shook his head. "Unlikely, since there is now little to divide, but someday the estate will be in better nick."

Vincent looked across at Caroline. "Hardwick forged a will that would have put him in charge of everything."

Roslyn gasped. "How did he think he could get away with that?"

Mark shrugged. "A crooked solicitor."

"But I have the will," Caroline said.

Mark and Vincent both stared at Caroline, gape-mouthed.

Vincent regained his breath just as Mark appeared in danger of laughing. Roslyn elbowed him.

"You—you have it?" Vincent stuttered. "Did you not think— Very well. Is it here?"

"Yes. I packed Luther's strongbox and only just recently found the key. Shall I run get it?"

Mark smiled. "No, please do not run upstairs just for that."

"Did it not occur to you…" Vincent started, but Mark shook his head.

"Had I known where you were going today, I would have sorted it out for you." Caroline's cheeks were pink with embarrassment.

"The real will may not help," Mark said, "but it would be as well to have it."

"Roslyn, it is in the wooden trunk," Caroline said, "and the key is in the lock."

Roslyn mastered the stairs and went into Caroline's room to throw open the trunk. There at the bottom was the strongbox that used to have a bit of money in it. Luther had made them beg for even a few pennies from its hoard. She hated the item for all the past evil memories of it. She brought it down and discovered that the family had moved to the library.

Mark pushed it toward Vincent. "You seem to be our expert on wills."

Vincent found the document and unfolded it. "No

cash bequests to anyone. Everything to go to his firstborn son. A little spartan, but it could be worse. Shall you take this round tomorrow, Mark?"

"Yes. Is there anything else in the box we should know about?"

"Some deeds…the one to the estate, of course, and the entailed lands, but also a deed to the smith shop, three houses in town, and if I am not mistaken, the deed to the Red Lion." He handed them over to Mark one at a time, and he passed them on to Caroline.

"There are also deeds to four parcels of land bordering the estate." Vincent laid them on the big table.

Mark shook his head as he scanned them. "These used to be freeholds and they have been turned into tenants."

"How did he come by these?" Vincent asked.

"Probably buying up debts or lending money," Thomas said.

"Luther had a terrible fight with Hardwick in the fall," Carolyn said. "Luther brought the box upstairs and hid it in my room. He warned me never to let Hardwick get his hands on it."

Elizabeth looked sad. "What a tangle."

"Thomas, make a list of everything for me to take round to the solicitor. But this is progress, I think."

Caroline was in tears. "What are we to do with these deeds? Don't you see? This is why everyone hated us so. This is where the money went."

"No doubt." Vincent placed them all back in the strongbox and handed it to Thomas.

Roslyn stood without knowing what she meant to say. "Give them all back."

Mark smiled up at her.

"I mean it. Give them all back. We can be sure that even if they were acquired legally, it was not right to do so."

"It is a brilliant solution, if Caroline agrees." Mark looked toward his sister-in-law seated on the sofa.

"Yes, when we return to Glassmere we will sign them over. By then we will know if I have the right to do that."

Thomas looked around the room. "Such a gesture would assure that you and the children will be loved in the district, so I almost hate to mention the one consideration that could be dangerous."

Roslyn nodded. "I know. We would possibly be handing property back to the person who killed Luther."

"Of course I thought of that," Caroline said proudly. "If it is not Hardwick, and we fail to figure out who it is, then that might placate them. And it would be just."

"I cannot argue with that," Elizabeth said. "Someday we will be able to enjoy ourselves without business intruding."

"Speaking of fun," Vincent said, "some friends of mine are getting up a party tomorrow for Vauxhall, and I thought Ros might like it. There is music, food, laughter, and lots of plantings and lanterns."

"I have never been there, of course. Is it safe?"

Vincent raised an eyebrow. "It is frequented by soldiers."

"That is no answer."

"I think you will like it," Mark said.

"You are all invited as well," Vincent added.

"I had rather stay home and rest, but I agree Roslyn deserves to get out. For now, I am going to bed with a somewhat quiet mind, knowing I can repair some of the damage caused by Luther."

"Let us go, then," Roslyn said as she got up to help Caroline to bed.

She felt optimistic herself, knowing the people around Glassmere would think better of Caroline. She was sure Caroline was right in thinking this was where the eight thousand pounds went. They had thought that not recoverable, and now it would go to a good cause.

She was proud of Caroline's decision, though it had been her idea. The weight of profiting by Luther's machinations would have tainted any value in the deeds. Mark was right. It was best to look for opportunities to help.

Chapter Eight

On their ride the next day, they ventured across the river to Green Park. Elizabeth had Mark drive her in the curricle so she could watch the girls riding and, Mark suspected, talk to him in private. There were many streets to negotiate to get there, but his team was well-mannered and calm, as were the riding horses. Tess chattered the whole way. With Vincent and Roslyn on either side of her, she seemed safe enough.

He realized he counted Roslyn as competent a protector for Tess as Vincent. And why not? She had kept the child safe far longer.

Elizabeth cleared her throat when they finally got to the park. "I thought this might not hurt your shoulder as much as riding."

He gave a small gasp. "Nearly healed anyway."

"Not an accident?"

"No. How could you tell?"

"The way you carry yourself."

"We did not want to worry Caroline, with the baby so close to coming."

"I perceive she is made of pretty stern stuff. Perhaps not as resourceful as Roslyn but with a good head on her shoulders."

"You are right. She deserves to know there is still a danger."

"I am sure after our conversation last night she

already perceives that. But I'm glad she is not going to Vauxhall. I do not fancy it much myself."

"We barely need the carriage. It cannot be more than ten minutes' drive, if you want to go and then return early."

"I have seen it enough times. I had rather be home knitting things with Caroline. I never had a daughter, so she is a joy to me. Roslyn as well. You are going to marry her, are you not?"

"I am trying. I have asked her, but she feels too much on guard."

"Hence your need to find the murderer."

"Yes, that does spur me on. I might have thought we did not need to know—until someone took a swipe at me on the bridge."

"You do not think they would back off if they knew you were letting it drop?"

"I have not taken action against anyone except Hardwick."

"Then if you can put him in jail, at least for embezzlement, that should make things safe."

"We may not be able to press that suit if the money was used to buy up debt. Hardwick may have been acting on Luther's orders, up to a point."

"Oh, bother. Why is everything so complicated?"

Mark had no answer for her, but his hands tightened on the reins when a thought bounded into his head.

"What is it?"

"Like an idiot, I lost my temper with Lord Raby and threatened him if he does not let Roslyn alone."

"Yes, I was there. Mark, you have a very long fuse, but when you do go off it is disastrous."

"He insisted that he should be given Roslyn's hand

in marriage to make up for Luther's gaming debts."

"That bounder, that cad! If I had him here I would wring his neck."

Mark chuckled. "I almost did. Happy to see I get my temper from you."

She laughed then. "I will deal with Raby. I have some power in society still."

Mark was glad he was not the unsuspecting lord.

\*\*\*\*

It was at lunch that Caroline broached the subject of a governess for Tess. Roslyn felt the suggestion like a stab in the heart. Of course there were things she could not teach Tess, but she thought she was competent on many subjects, especially the pianoforte. Since the dressmaker was coming to fit their costumes for the soiree and Thomas was doing math lessons with Tess, Roslyn occupied herself with her musical selections. At least she could do that, but she could not get over the feeling Caroline was trying to push her away.

They ate dinner at home that night since the fare at Vauxhall would be light. Unwilling to borrow something nice from Elizabeth, Roslyn wore her only evening gown, though it was old. None of the new gowns were ready yet. On the way in the carriage Vincent mentioned, "They are planning to reenact Waterloo at Vauxhall if they can get a thousand men."

"But why?" Roslyn asked. "I mean why would they not want to forget it?"

"I cannot explain, but it was the most significant event of our generation."

Mark looked puzzled. "But Vincent, who would play the French? No one would want to."

"A job for raw recruits."

By the time they got to the box rented by Vincent, his friends had imbibed wine freely and not had dinner yet. Several of them wanted to walk Roslyn along the secluded pathways, but Vincent reserved that right for himself, though Roxby and Turpin decided to trail along.

Mark raised an inquiring eyebrow.

Roslyn smiled. "I'm sure I will be fine."

"So Vincent is in charge of the estate now?" Captain Tillby asked.

Mark poured himself a bit of wine and relaxed. "He has agreed to handle Cahill property since I am tied up with my shipping business."

"I am happy he has some employment. Frankly, I was worried about him after the war was over. Too much time on his hands. He fell in with some bad company."

"My brother, in fact." Mark smiled to soften the comment.

"I was going to say Raby, but your brother as well."

"Because Vincent was keeping an eye on his sisters and niece. I am thankful for that."

"Too bad Cahill did not turn up his toes before he ruined the place— Sorry, should not have said that."

"It is a common sentiment. Between us we have the time and skills to bring the place back before the new Lord Cahill inherits it."

"Excellent. I am glad to see Vincent doing so well."

They talked then of the war and the economy afterward. Tillby mentioned the three men of the party were landed gentry but not equally wealthy. They all had trouble getting their places set to rights and resuming the more mundane duties of a gentleman.

"I hear you dismissed your estate agent."

"Vincent can take care of all that now."

Roslyn and the rest came back just as the food arrived. All of the men seemed falling all over each other to get her slices of ham or peel oranges for her. Her face was pink over all the attention, and she laughed more than Mark had ever heard her laugh before. Then the music started, and she was rapt.

"Like food, music is much more wonderful outdoors," she whispered to him.

The air was cool, but the soldiers gave off enough heat that she did not seem to need her cloak. When the evening drew to a close, Vincent said, "Take the carriage without me. I promised to go see Cargill for a bit. I am told he is under the hatches. Or I suppose it is not proper—"

Roslyn grasped his sleeve. "Vincent. We have the carriage with a coachman and footman. It will be fine. Thank you for a wonderful evening."

Mark shook Vincent's hand as the other men fell over each other to hold her cloak for her. "How did you know she needed this so much, to be admired and courted?" he whispered to Vincent.

"She has never been, you know. It is not fair."

As they walked to the carriage, Mark took her arm.

"How wonderful," she said. "I feel sated with music, lights, greenery, and conversation, though I think it is highly dangerous for you to be walking in the night. Not everyone could know you have no desire to be Lord Cahill."

"Why do you think I cowered at the pavilion?"

"I think to give me a night of freedom."

Their coach pulled out of line and came to the edge of the walkway as though the coachman had been watching for them. Mark helped her in and sat opposite.

"I suppose it is improper for me to escort you alone, but we will be home in a few minutes." He kicked down the drop seat on the right door and rested a foot on it.

"All those soldiers—they do not want to forget," she said in amazement.

"It was a great moment in history. We should not forget it either."

She pressed her hands to her cheeks. "It was agony, and so many of them died or had life-changing wounds."

"I know. I do not understand…"

"What is it?" she asked at his concerned look.

"The coachman is not going the right way. He passed the street we would normally take."

"Oh, no! And it was such a wonderful evening. What are you doing?" she asked as Mark put his head out the window.

"Seeing who it is." Mark levered himself out the window and climbed up onto the top.

Roslyn heard a struggle and two bodies slamming into the roof. He was fighting with either the footman or the coachman. Possibly no one was driving the team.

She threw the right door open and the wind slammed it against the coach. Looking forward, she saw reins trailing.

She stepped on the drop seat on the door and heard her gown split up the left leg, so she tore it the rest of the way and climbed up to grasp the roof rack. Then a shadow, the fake footman, climbed from the boot onto the roof, toward Mark, with a dagger. Just as he stood, she grabbed his ankle and yanked. He slammed into the roof and bounced off onto the ground with a thud and a grunt.

If she could get to the box, she might stop the coach,

but it was more important to help Mark, who was now wrestling with a huge opponent. Using the drop seat and then the door sill as a purchase, she managed with more tearing of muslin to crawl onto the top of the coach. When she saw a knife drawn, she grabbed her own knife from her cloak pocket and stabbed what she could reach, the back of the man's thigh. His howl of rage was followed by Mark kicking him off with first one foot and then the other.

Roslyn ducked so the huge body would not take her with it. Then Mark grabbed her by the wrist and pulled her toward the box.

He was clutching his right arm to his side, so she crawled forward and snatched the only rein that whipped her way. Even tugging on just that seemed to slow the team a bit.

Mark knelt and leaned down to grab another, but could not reach any.

"I shall have to ride post on one of them, the left horse, I think, since you have a rein for the right one. The inside reins are both broken."

She held her breath as he got on the traces, then leaped for the back of the horse. With only one arm, he almost slid under the wheels, but he righted himself and got hold of the short outside rein. She held the outside rein for the other horse, so together they were able to turn the team.

Slowly they brought them down to a walk.

"Turn them right at the next street."

"It is a left after that, is it not?"

"Correct. I fear for our coachman and footman."

"I do as well, and all for a night's pleasure."

"Never think this was your fault. I should have been

more observant."

With him on one horse and her steering the other, they got the team back to the stable yard. She pulled her cloak over her ruined skirt as she hopped down from the driver's seat.

"My lord!" The head groom looked astonished to see her getting down from the box.

"Some of you go search for Geoff Coachman and Nick, the footman," Mark ordered. "They may have been killed."

"They just staggered in. Someone knocked Geoff out while Nick was gone. When he came back, the coach was gone. He brought Geoff home in a hackney."

"Send for a doctor for him."

"He is on the way."

"My lord, have you taken an injury?" The head groom caught the bits of the team.

"Nothing serious. The horses broke half the reins, which means they may have cut their mouths with the bits."

"We shall take care of them, sir."

By the time she got Mark upstairs, his coat was drenched and her dress blood-soaked, but it was in tatters anyway. She was glad the focus of the staff was in the stable yard. The rest of the household seemed to have gone to bed, though Thomas might still be up.

"I go through more linen this way." Mark sat on the bed.

"Stop complaining and let me see."

"What are the damages?"

"He has raked your ribs and the inside of your forearm."

"Does not sound bad, though it burns like fire."

"I have some ointment. Hold this toweling between your arm and side. I'll be right back."

While in her room, she stepped out of her destroyed gown and put on a wrapper, then got her lint bandages and salve.

"There was blood on your dress. Are you injured?"

"That was from our would-be coachman."

"Where did you get him?"

"In the leg."

"Good for you, though I wish you had not been pressed to defend yourself. And do you usually carry a knife in your pocket to social engagements?"

"Vincent gave me the dagger years ago, before he went off to war. He never thought we were safe but could do no more than that at the time."

"Thank God he was not with us."

Roslyn tilted her head at him. "But he might have helped."

"He might have been killed." Mark took a drink of brandy.

"I know it looks suspicious."

"I mean they were probably prepared to stab him to death and leave him there. They wanted all our bodies at some distance or not found at all."

She was relieved and shocked at the same time. Mark did not blame Vincent, yet had no illusions about what would have happened to them. "He will be upset."

"He is a soldier. He is used to this sort of thing."

By the time she had taped his ribs and bandaged his arm, Mark could move without grunting. She left the salve and went to her own room to lean against the closed door with a sigh. Mark was the one who was apt to be killed. Why both of them? She owned nothing, would inherit nothing. The answer came. She would have been a witness.

It was just too bad. That had been her favorite gown…because it was her only gown. At least it was not a new one, but her new slippers and stockings were ruined.

Suddenly she started laughing and slid down against the door. How inured she had become to emergencies, to weigh a new pair of slippers against her life or that of Mark.

Chapter Nine

It rained the next morning, and Mark was almost glad. It would give him a chance to rest, though he meant to go down to breakfast. He had heard Roslyn's almost maniacal laugh last night and had meant to go to her but fell asleep in his clothes.

When Jarvis the footman brought him shaving water, he promoted him to valet on condition he would take care of Thomas's gear as well. The man was overcome with pride and gratitude. Mark asked about the coachman. Jarvis said he was recovering.

"Send a messenger to the magistrate. We cannot let this go unreported."

After he shaved and had Jarvis help him with a shirt, coat, and neck cloth, he went to the breakfast parlor to find everyone eating, drinking tea, and staring out the window. Tess was disappointed about the rain after her daily success at riding.

"I am going to take some biscuits to my horse," she said waiting to have someone dissuade her.

"Wear a cloak," was all Caroline said.

"And go no farther than the stable," Thomas warned before Mark could say it. He smiled at Thomas and clumsily got a plate of food for himself. Roslyn got up for more tea and poured him a cup of coffee.

"Thank you."

"Vincent is usually here by now," Caroline said.

Mark stopped himself from shrugging or moving his torso at all. "He may not come, since we are not to ride."

Roslyn glanced at him. "We have had more than our share of fair days."

"Probably means extra school lessons." Tess pouted as she gathered some biscuits up in a napkin.

"Or more time to play with your kitten," Caroline answered.

Tess smiled and left.

"What sort of place is London becoming when a coachman is attacked?" Elizabeth demanded.

"It ever was dangerous," Mark said.

Vincent came in and stared at Mark, then Roslyn. "Is it true? Was your carriage attacked last night?"

Roslyn cleared her throat. "Not so much attacked as stolen."

"But they say you drove it back, you and Roslyn."

"It took two of us because half the reins were broken." She buttered a scone as though it was her chief interest.

"So how did you get rid of the thieves?"

Roslyn took a bite, possibly to add to the suspense. "One fell off the roof."

Mark smiled. "The other Roslyn stabbed with that dagger you gave her."

Vincent gaped and everyone else stared at him.

She glared at him, then seemed angry. "I ruined my favorite gown and my new slippers."

Mark laughed, even though it made his ribs hurt.

Vincent rested his hand on a chair back. "If I'd had any inkling…"

"We have the magistrate coming," Mark said. "The most serious injury is to the coachman. He may not be able to drive for some time. But then we need new reins."

"Sit down, Vincent, and eat something." Lady Cahill motioned. "After a time, you will not be shocked at anything that happens in this family."

Thomas shook his head. "I slept through the whole thing. I was working in the library and passed out over a pile of contracts."

Mark grinned. "I hope you did not drool on them."

"No, they are fine, but I have a terrible crick in my neck."

Vincent had finally got coffee and food from the sideboard. "I planned to go to Bath today to hunt for our aunt. That sounds so tame compared to your evening."

"I do not know if we can spare you just yet," Roslyn said.

Mark nodded. "In light of this attack, I think not."

"I want to cover the ground of the attack last night. I lost my dagger, the one you gave me, and I want it back," Roslyn put in.

"We had better go early then," Vincent said. "Who will give Tess lessons today?"

"I will," her grandmother said. "She should learn a bit about my London. We will make use of that map."

****

They took the curricle, with a footman up behind to hold the team when they stopped. Roslyn directed him backward over the route they had followed, and sure enough, they saw the handle of her dagger glinting at the side of the open stretch of road where the struggle had been the most intense.

Vincent recovered it and whistled. "The bloodstain goes halfway up the blade. You may have done for that fellow."

"I certainly hope so. Mark is pretty sure they meant to kill us and dump us in the Thames."

"Why would they harm *you*?"

"I might be able to identify them. Of course they must not have guessed I could get up onto the top of the coach and attack. I got out and stood on the window sill to boost myself up."

He came and hugged his sister. "Poor Roslyn. Always fighting in the last ditch. I could have prevented this."

She looked up at him and shook her head slowly. "Mark said they probably would have killed you first, before we left the gardens."

"I see. Get rid of three protectors at once."

"The one playing coachman landed here, where I lost my knife."

Vincent kicked about in the weeds and finally came up with another knife.

"What is it?" she asked.

"I don't recall seeing the like. We can ask Mark if he recognizes it."

They got back in and proceeded in the direction of Vauxhall.

"I think the one playing footman fell on this stretch."

Once again Vincent combed the area beside the road, but it was their footman who spotted the weapon and pointed to a ditch on the other side of the road.

"An army dirk. This means we may have ex-soldiers involved."

"Who would be able to hire them?"

"Me or anyone like me. Scum of the earth, some of them. But no pensions. What are they to do?"

"Poverty is no excuse for murder."

"I will put off the trip to Bath. It's probably a fool's errand anyway."

"Wait until after the soiree. This search cannot be so desperate as the one to find a Cahill heir."

"I agree, and I have kept you out in the cold and damp long enough. Why did I ever leave you?" Vincent asked.

"You were helping a friend, a common impulse between you and Mark. The two of you get on well because you are so much alike in your thinking."

"I know why I am as I am. I cannot imagine what has made him so foolish."

Roslyn smiled sadly. "He may tell us someday."

"Have you told him…about you?"

"No, but I think I shall have to if he asks me to marry him again."

Vincent took an audible breath. "He would never care what you have been through."

"I fear he may care too much."

\*\*\*\*

Mark asked Roslyn to be present when they spoke to the magistrate. The man heard the start of the story from the coachman and footman, then dismissed them and turned to a clean page in his notebook.

He seemed aghast when the three weapons were laid before him, hearing Mark out first before getting confirmation of the story from Roslyn. Mark had the impression he did not believe them.

"So the two of you managed to thwart both thieves and drive the coach home."

"We were lucky," Mark said.

"So I am looking for a shorter man—possibly a discharged soldier—and a taller man with a limp."

"Or a corpse with a leg wound," Roslyn said.

The magistrate stared at her, then got out his handkerchief to gather up the weapons.

"No, I am keeping mine." She picked it up and held it to the light. "It was a gift."

The man cleared his throat. "I will contact you if anything turns up."

Mark bit his lip in an effort not to laugh, at least not until the man was shown out, for it would hurt his ribs.

"Are you in pain?" Vincent asked.

"No," Mark choked out, shaking his head.

Roslyn pursed her lips. "You know he does not plan to help us anyway."

Vincent choked on a laugh. "That was no reason to terrify him."

Mark heard the outer door close and let out his chuckle. "Ow. Now I am in pain."

"No more than you deserve," Roslyn said.

Vincent gritted his teeth. "You two will be the death of me...or yourselves."

"How bad is your wound?" she asked.

"Superficial, unless I get an infection from that boning knife."

"Any of your seamen have a grudge against you?" Vincent asked.

"They are probably all still drunk."

"Still, keep wary of them."

"It will have to be the Bow Street Runners after all," Mark announced.

"May I come when you hire them?" Roslyn asked.

"No," the men said in unison.

"Don't you have lessons for Tess tomorrow?"

"They are interviewing the new governess

tomorrow."

Mark blinked. "Perhaps you should come with us."

"What are you afraid I will do?"

Vincent rubbed his forehead. "I think Mark is trying to choose the lesser of two confrontations."

"I was just joking. I shall spend tomorrow practicing my pieces for the soiree."

"I keep forgetting that party," Mark said. "That settles it. We need two Runners in the house before that night."

At dinner, they discussed where they were with everything. Thomas, Caroline, and Elizabeth wanted to know.

"The magistrate seemed to regard the attack last night as a random robbery," Mark said.

"That's ridiculous," Caroline said. "They never asked for money."

"An unsuccessful robbery," Vincent said, "since Roslyn and Mark recovered the team and carriage. We are on our own with this."

Mark thought for a minute. "Since the kidnapping and murder was also unsuccessful, he can list this as a crime solved. Vincent and I shall definitely hire some Runners tomorrow. Always wanted to see how those fellows worked."

"It would not hurt to have an extra guard at the house. Do you have guards on the warehouse where your office is?" Vincent asked.

"Two at all times."

"So once you are there, you are safe."

"So far. Thomas can guard the house tomorrow until we get more help."

Thomas groaned. "For the soiree we will have a

hundred strangers in and out of here with flowers and food. I shall go daft! And who is to go to the office?"

"We will stop there on our way back," Mark replied.

Vincent pushed his plate aside. "We can make use of Evers for tomorrow, at least. Since we now have a groom, butler, cook, and maid at the town house, I am not worried about Hardwick invading."

"Is he in town, then?" Caroline asked.

Roslyn nodded. "So far as we know."

"But he was not one of the ruffians who attacked you?" Thomas asked.

Roslyn shook her head. "I would have recognized him. That does not mean he did not hire them."

Thomas swept a hand across his eyes. "Your double negative is blurring my mind. I must go draft some bills of lading and export papers for the next ship to go out. Also order provisions, which you and Mark must see to tomorrow."

"I need all your paperwork by nine in the morning."

"I shall be up all night then. Fortunately, I brought the inventory of the warehouse with me so I know what we have to sell."

"The *Camille* has been completely unloaded," Mark said. "Here is the warehoused list."

"Good thing you brought this. I shall get to work now." Thomas left the room without ceremony.

"Thank you, Mark, for ruining another evening," his mother said.

"It is hard to run a business from your house."

"Impossible without Thomas," she agreed.

"Shall I tell him now I plan to make him a partner?"

Caroline gave a slight smile. "I am not sure he would thank you for that right now."

Vincent laughed and refused the port. "Roslyn, I heard I was to be treated to a preview of tomorrow night's performance."

"My part anyway," Roslyn said.

Mark stood and pulled Roslyn to her feet. "I want to hear it as well, in case we are too busy tomorrow night to listen."

"Too busy doing what, Mark?" his mother asked. But Mark did not answer her.

So far as Mark could tell, Roslyn's playing was flawless, and he hoped Thomas, busy in the next room, took a moment to appreciate it, since he was the musician. Moreover, Roslyn's performance was passionate. Now he realized under that cold and calculating warrior-maiden exterior beat a heart full of emotions and, he hoped, joy. It meant his suit was not hopeless.

Chapter Ten

The next day, Vincent caught Mark alone in the library just after breakfast. He was signing documents after a brief perusal, but he trusted Thomas to make iron-clad contracts.

"I must tell you something," Vincent confided.

"Yes?" Mark looked up and smiled.

"The reason I left you two nights before last was that my second captain, Compton, was sure Lieutenant Cargill was going to kill himself."

"My God! After surviving Waterloo?" Mark cast the pen aside and stood.

"He lost an arm, so his military career is over. The rest of us had a place to come back to. Or in my case I have family. He has nothing, no one."

"We must do something." Mark began to pace.

"I offered him the agent position at Glassmere."

"That will work. He can even live in the wing where the office is. It will give you more time with family, and you won't have to run back and forth so much."

Vincent bit his lip. "I did it without consulting you."

Mark chuckled. "Do you imagine you need my permission to make these decisions, especially when the solution is so obvious?"

"He has absolutely no qualifications."

"Except leading a troop of soldiers into the most deadly battle in recent history. I imagine riding herd on

Glassmere will be a walk in the park after that."

Vincent shrugged. "Another expenditure."

"What good is money if we do not spend it? The shipping business will support the estate until it is in better frame. The crops this year were better. It all takes time. Will he be all right by himself? He will have the company of the tenants and grooms in the daytime and the house staff at night. He might even wish to marry someday. Glassmere would be the perfect place to raise a family."

"It was lack of employment that wrenched his soul so. I thought to take him up there and introduce him myself, but that would have seemed…"

"As though you were worried about him, when he is capable of getting there himself with the proper letter of introduction."

"And the incentive to do something," Vincent added. "I gave him some of your sovereigns and a letter of introduction to the staff."

"Perfect." Mark rubbed his hands together and resumed his seat. "I like people free and willing to act. Free will is the greatest gift we have ever been given."

Vincent sat on the edge of the desk as Mark tidied his documents. "You are an odd sort of fellow to know."

Mark looked up. "I could say the same about you. Let us go hire those Runners, then drop off this paperwork."

\*\*\*\*

The interview at Bow Street seemed more matter-of-fact than Mark had expected. There was a contract to be signed for the two Runners, who would take turns guarding the house, and for the detective, who would look into his brother's death plus do some research in

Bath that Vincent wanted done. It all seemed like such a normal transaction Mark felt quite comfortable with it.

The drive to the warehouse took some time, during which Vincent seemed to be brooding.

"What's wrong?" Mark asked.

"It occurs to me once again that my family is costing you a great deal of money."

"I happen to be lucky enough to spend my money on things that make more money without my really intending to. It all evens out."

Vincent laughed. "So how did you accidentally make a fortune?"

"I started out with one ship financed by Mother, and I invested in books to carry to America. A friend of hers in Boston steered me to the porcelain trade. You see, about fifty years ago a British potter named John Bartlam set up a manufacture in South Carolina because of the abundance of clay. I buy from the pottery factories there, and they do not risk breakage in wagon transport to the north. We pack the goods in barrels of rice and haul them north to Philadelphia, Boston, and New York. Sometimes Nova Scotia. We fill the rest of the ship with teak and mahogany to carry north."

"No cotton?"

"Not if we can avoid it. Besides being made entirely on the backs of slaves, if it gets wet you have a horrid mess."

"Trading up the American coast you pay no import duties," Vincent said in surprise.

"Right. I can give buyers a better price than if the dishes came from England. If we offload most of the goods at those ports, we take on whatever we think will sell in the next destination."

"And for the return trip?"

"Whatever we have left, plus hardwood lumber."

"You go nowhere else?"

"We sometimes take tin goods and other manufactured articles to South America and Cuba and load on coffee and more exotic woods. One of our captains is skillful at that trade, but he finishes with the Eastern Seaboard run. The third ship goes to Europe, and Africa if there is a need for lace, silks, and other textiles."

"And it all works like a well-oiled machine."

"Surprisingly so. Of course, we cannot schedule when the ships will arrive to switch cargoes, hence the large brick warehouse to store things."

"You do not go on every ship."

"I have made all three runs to scope out trade agreements, but no, there are three ships, all with their own captains. I am most likely to sail on the *Venture* to the American seaboard. The *Shark* makes the extended run to South America when we need coffee stores. The *Camille* goes to Europe to carry the remnants of what we bring back from America to Belgium, France, Spain, and possibly Africa, picking up lace, wine, and finished leather goods."

Vincent chuckled again. "If it was not your intention to make money, what was it?"

"Something interesting to do, seeing how many people I can employ, setting up the well-oiled machine."

They pulled up to St. Savior's quay on the south side of the Thames to much activity.

"The *Camille* is almost ready to sail, filling water barrels now and ready to take on stores."

"The cargo?" Vincent asked.

"Books, coffee, wood, some tinware, and even some

rice and porcelain, almost all loaded. They will embark the day after tomorrow."

While Mark conferred with a clerk in the busy yard and handed him money for the stores, Vincent stood and watched the loading of barrels by two strong black dock workers.

"Freemen?" he asked as they went in the door.

"Now they are." Mark threw over his shoulder.

Vincent followed him upstairs to the office. "Do you—how do you stand on abolition?"

"I am for it, of course. It is the law." Mark sensed that Vincent had guessed about their contraband.

Vincent sat in one of the side chairs and sighed. "In England, not in America. And I suppose if slaves swim out to your ship, say, in the Carolinas, you are going to help them escape."

Mark threw up his hands. "Of course." As though no other decision could be possible.

"And what do your seamen think of this?"

"The captains are all abolitionists. The seamen do not care, but most are sympathetic."

Vincent stared at him in wonder. "I am speechless."

"At my generosity? It costs me little. It is not as though we are putting out passengers."

"No, at your audacity. I mean, here you are scratching your head over who is trying to kill you, and the most likely candidate is some slave owner."

"Oh." Mark thought for a moment. "I *am* an idiot."

"You must have brought a *slave taker* back from your last voyage." Vincent used the term as though he referred to the filthiest vermin on earth, then got up and paced to the window.

"We did take on a crewman in Charleston when one

of ours absconded. I had not thought of that."

"Obviously."

Mark leaned back in his chair and ruminated. "So we have two puzzles to solve."

"Is that all you can say?" Vincent came back to tower over him.

"Well, it simplifies matters."

"How does it?" Vincent almost shouted with exasperation as he leaned on the desk.

"This may mean that your sisters and Tess are safe. No one has acted specifically against them since we came to town. As for me, I can take care of myself."

"Apparently not. From the way Roslyn describes the fight on top of the carriage, you would have been killed, without her assistance. And do you really think my sister will be overjoyed that only *your* life is in danger?"

Mark bit his bottom lip, then looked up at Vincent. "Perhaps we should not tell them."

Vincent shook his head. "I leave that to you. But they would have killed Roslyn without compunction. I think everyone around you is in grave danger."

"You are right. They need to know even if it worries them."

"Are the current escapees here or at the house?"

"Here, on the fourth floor. They ship out on the *Camille*, departing in two days. So we only have to be on guard two days."

"On their behalf. Even if you stop this reverse slave-running, the slavers *will* still kill you."

"Then it is a good thing you are here."

Vincent smacked himself on the forehead. "You are hopeless."

"You may visit with the free family if you like while

I take these documents to Captain Sellick. Then we can go home."

"Where are they bound for, these freemen?"

"Most usually want to get to Canada, though some stay in England, others France. But this family wants to go home—Africa. He is a chief there."

Vincent did start up the stairs rather than down them, and Mark trusted that conversing with the escaped slaves would whet Vincent's ready sympathy.

Chapter Eleven

Roslyn voted against riding the next morning since everyone had so much to do. Even Tess was having her new dress altered so she could be in the receiving line. She did not care to sit through the music, which she had heard many times. Besides, she would be able to hear it from her bedroom.

Roslyn found Mark in the library. It seemed an oasis of calm in a household where everyone else had run mad. Mark seemed strangely calm when she reported, "Vincent's batman is conferring with a Runner, I suppose about security, while maids are dashing about with linen and glassware and footmen are placing baskets of flowers around the hall, drawing room, and music room wherever Caroline commands."

"Where is Mother?" he asked.

"Helping with Tess's fitting. Thomas must be at the office." She realized Mark had been staring at her and waiting to know what she wanted.

He smiled. "This is probably the only place where a person could hear herself think and that is only because Thomas has discovered more in the inventory that can be shipped and has driven off to see to the paperwork."

"There is something I must tell you."

"Before the musical?"

"No—yes. Something I should have told you before. I feel I am living here under false pretenses."

"What can it be?" Mark stood up and came to her.

"Someone was after me when I was young."

"When you were a child." He led her to the sofa and waited for her to sit before he rested beside her.

"Hardly. I was sixteen. It was the spoiled son of our agent."

"The one who ruined your estate."

"Yes, that one." She stopped wringing her handkerchief and looked him in the eyes. "I was throwing hay down for our few horses, and he cornered me in the loft."

Mark opened his mouth but said nothing and took her hands.

"By the time Vincent rode in...before he..." she faltered.

Mark kissed her forehead and held her. "I understand."

"When Vincent rode in, it was too late, but he was like an enraged bull as he came up the ladder. I kicked at the villain and he stumbled off the edge. He broke his back when he fell."

"I am so sorry. But this explains why you are such a good fighter."

She sucked in an unsteady breath. "I would have killed him on purpose."

"As would I. Are you both safe from inquiry?" Mark asked.

"Vincent got me to the house. It was dark by then. He must have made the man's clothes right and laid the pitchfork beside him. That is how they found him in the morning. There was no inquiry."

"I have ever been a fan of swift justice." He felt her tense, so released her and took her cold hands in his.

"So if I seem distant to you, unable to accept your attentions, there is a reason."

"I will indeed understand, but that does not mean I will give up courting you. Just because the past has been horrible for both of us does not mean the future will be."

"Oh, Mark. We do not even know if we have a future."

He kissed her cheek and gave her his handkerchief to blot her tears.

"Of course we have. We just have to find my brother's murderer, trap the assassins who are after me, make sure we hobble Raby, and bring Hardwick to justice."

She chuckled. "Oh, well, here I was thinking it was complicated."

"Of course, I hope for some overlap in those tasks."

She sniffed. "If they are four separate tasks, it may just take a bit longer."

"Have I ever told you how much I admire you?" he asked.

"Why?" She sniffed and stared at him.

"You have never abandoned your post, never had a thought for yourself."

"There are many like me."

"But most at least wish for a life of their own."

"I have a life. I love Caroline and Tess. Soon there will be a baby to love. I don't see why we need two nursery maids and a governess."

"You don't like Mrs. Trent?"

"I don't dislike her, but I can give Tess her lessons as before."

"Tess likes Mrs. Trent."

"Because you hired her."

"Actually, Caroline decided Tess needed a governess and Vincent found her."

"Found? It sounds as though she was lost."

"Before I address that, do you have any quarrel with her qualifications?"

"Her French is better than mine, she plays the pianoforte as well as I do, and she is an expert at watercolor. Does this sound like a case of jealousy?"

"She is also the widow of a major lost at Waterloo but not found dead. She is now struggling to live, since a pension has not been awarded."

"Oh, I am sad for her. Presumed dead but not proven. So you and Vincent rescued her."

"We prefer to think of it as putting her skills to good use."

"Then I withdraw my objection, since she is in need."

"She is deserving."

"What shame is there to be in need? You rescued all of us."

Mark sighed and laughed. "You did not need me. I venture you would have soon writ to the lawyers demanding they settle the estate. Once you figured out Hardwick was hobbling the mail, you would have dealt with everything much as I did. Confess. You had some such plan in mind."

"Of course. I cannot go to sleep at night unless I have a plan."

"The other consideration is that Caroline wants you to have your freedom, not to be chained to her and Tess through need but only by love. She believes you can find other occupations than caring for Tess. Perhaps even find time to marry and have children yourself?"

Roslyn gave him a suspicious look. "Are you asking me again to marry you?"

"Well, *yes.*"

"Even though we have not solved who is trying to harm us?"

"We may never find out."

"We have to. We cannot live like this."

"Very well. Once we bring everyone to justice, I will ask you again. Now, I think you want to practice your pieces before Thomas returns."

As Roslyn left the library, Vincent saw him standing in the open door and came in.

"What is it?" Mark asked.

"As you requested, I went to Captain Barlow to see if he could locate the crewman who signed on during the last voyage. The seaman has disappeared."

Mark nodded. "Not that unusual when in port, but most of the men come back to sleep on the ship so they do not miss a departure and lose their berth."

"Perhaps the Runners can track him down."

Mark nodded. "I think we need to hire more of them."

Vincent turned to go, then came back. "Roslyn told you the whole? She said she would."

"Yes, I am very proud of both of you. You did the only thing possible to help her."

"If he had survived the fall, I probably would have just beaten him to death."

"Of course."

"What happened was not her fault. She did everything she could to avoid him."

"Vincent, if the fellow were still alive, I'd kill him myself. Nothing she told me makes me love her less. I still want to marry her. I just know now why she is so reluctant to trust."

"It was not just that incident. If you knew how many times she had to hold Raby off with a poker. And Luther would not stop him."

"Our family has a lot to answer for."

"Hard to believe you were brothers."

Mark tilted his head. "I'm not entirely sure about that."

"What?"

"Just a niggling suspicion that I am not my father's son. I do not look like either my father or my brother. Mother sent me away from there as soon as she could—sent me to America to be mentored by a man I do look like. He taught me navigation and advised me how to set myself up in trade."

"This is why you are hoping Caroline will have a son."

"One of several reasons. I have had a letter from Hardwick threatening dire consequences if I do not return the will, the one he forged, and if I do not stop prosecuting him."

"You think he knows."

"If I figured it out, he would be as sharp."

"You could always ask your mother."

Mark shrugged. "More fun this way."

Vincent blew out a breath and raised his gaze just as Thomas tramped downstairs in evening clothes with a stiff look, running his finger around under his collar.

"Here I am, not even late, in evening clothes as ordered."

Mark smiled. "You look as though you are about to be strangled by that neck cloth."

"Jarvis tied it, but it is what I found out with my research that bothers me."

"What?" Mark asked.

"Come into the library, both of you." Thomas poured himself a brandy and downed it in one gulp, which was extraordinary behavior for him. "There is only one other close male relative."

Mark leaned on the desk. "Why are you so upset? Who is he?"

"You know I was adopted and a charity student?"

"And the top of your class. You could be managing a bank, but what does that have to do with it?"

"Managing a bank? Not without connections."

Vincent poured himself a drink. "You stray from the point. Have you found a connection?"

"As per the St. John family, yes. I am Mark's half-brother and therefore belong on the list of suspects."

Mark stared at Thomas, then came and embraced him. "But this is amazing."

"I feel as though I should give notice."

"Thomas, why? I am most happy for the connection."

"But I have a motive for killing Luther."

Vincent started to laugh and shake his head.

Mark gaped and then grinned. "That presupposes you knew about it before he was murdered, and you did not."

"Oh, that's right. I did not know I had a motive."

Vincent pulled himself together. "This will not keep you from offering for Caroline, will it?"

"No, but I would never presume…"

Vincent clapped him on the back. "I really think you should. She enjoys your company."

"Thomas, I was going to make you a partner anyway." Mark poured himself a brandy to celebrate the announcement. "In fact, I put that bit of legal work forward just in case I did get killed."

"Don't say that. You should be more careful. There have been two attempts on your life already."

"Yes, but we have the Runners with us now. Catch anyone trying to stab me with those fellows on watch." Mark wondered why Thomas was not delighted.

Chapter Twelve

Tess, in her blue muslin with gray ribbons, did her duty and greeted everyone, standing alongside Mark, Elizabeth, Vincent, Caroline, and Roslyn. Mark noticed the ladies were all in subdued shades of silk, his mother in lavender. Then Tess retired to her room to play with her kitten and listen from above, which she told Mark would be more fun than sitting quietly for two hours.

Thomas seemed stressed, and not by his upcoming performance. He refused to stand in the receiving line until he was properly married to Caroline, and kept himself busy managing the arrangement of the music room and the sorting of music.

The guests were served champagne and appetizers from trays as they gathered in the hall and music room. Afterward they would be released into the dining room, where a buffet of sea foods and ham, exotic fruits, and elaborate glacées and desserts was being assembled. The dining chairs and all the spare chairs in the house had been pulled into the music room to provide enough seats. After the music, of course, guests could wander about the downstairs while nibbling and conversing.

The thought of an entire night of this gave Mark a headache. "Mother, did you invite all these people?"

"No, some brought guests. If we are showing the girls off to get them into society, I do not want you throwing out the ones with no invitation cards."

Mark chuckled. "Damn, and I was so looking forward to punting Lord Raby down the steps."

"Is he here?" She craned her neck to look for him from the front row, but the chairs were all filled now.

Mark was beginning to feel trapped. "Probably lurking about somewhere, trying to importune Roslyn again."

"Quiet now—the music."

Thomas started with a lively piece and Roslyn turned the pages for him. He would do the same for her when she played, since Elizabeth was the only other person who could read music.

Mark did his best to keep an eye on the hall and the passage of guests to and from the refreshment salon while still enjoying Roslyn's playing. At least while she was at the pianoforte Raby could not accost her. Thomas and Roslyn alternated for several pieces. Then they did a vocal duet. Lady Pierce then sang a short aria while Thomas played.

By then Mark did not think absenting himself would matter. After all, he might be checking on the punch. He slipped out of his seat and toured the first floor. He spotted Raby in a doorway to the library, which would have unsettled him if he had not locked up all their documents about the investigation. Raby made for the refreshment salon, but Mark cornered him in the hallway and grabbed his arm.

"They are done playing."

Mark glared at him. "From the applause I would say so."

"You cannot keep me from seeing her."

"I can if I kill you, and I did promise to do that if you invaded this house again."

"If you do not let me marry Roslyn, I shall tell everyone you are illegitimate."

"Now I wonder where you got that idea."

"It is spoken of by many."

Mark shrugged. "So tell, if it is such common gossip."

"You cannot mean that."

"I am sure they will consider the source."

"Once I say it, it cannot be unsaid," Raby whispered.

"And I suppose I am to call you out over it?"

"That would be the gentlemanly thing to do."

Mark laughed. "You just said I am no such thing. I am surprised, since a knife in the back is more your method."

Mark saw a look of puzzlement cross Raby's face.

"I do not know what you are talking about, but your reputation hangs by a thread," Raby said.

"I will not duel with you in some antiquated show of honor. I will meet you face to face and beat you until you are dead or wish you were. And if you live, I will sue you for slander." Mark took a breath and relaxed his grip on Raby's coat sleeve. "But not tonight at Mother's soiree. It would upset her."

Raby had closed his eyes but opened them wide now at the sudden change in tone. Mark smoothed the man's lapels. "Now, get out."

Vincent was standing in the hall laughing as Raby stalked off. "Are you drunk?"

"Not drunk enough to suffer such fools."

"He may be a fool, but he is an expert shot."

"Only to be expected that a card cheat would be good at sleight of hand."

Vincent's face went serious. "Do not tell me you

accused him of that."

"Actually, I did once, and in the presence of a witness, Roslyn, but I figure since he did not call me out then, he accepted the accusation."

"Do not bank on it."

Mark was surprised how good it felt to toss the annoying card sharp out again. After that, he was politeness itself to the guests as they enjoyed victuals, good wine, and discussion. Eventually they all took themselves off and his mother relaxed into a chair in the drawing room.

"Well, Caroline, did you enjoy yourself?" she asked.

"Oh, yes! I have met so many people. How will I keep the names straight?"

"I have made notes," Roslyn said.

Vincent laughed as he tossed off a brandy.

Roslyn scanned her neat handwriting. "We had some here who were not invited: Lords Corbin, Bishoff, and Raby. Oh, and a funny man in tweeds I could not place."

"That is one of our Runners."

"Oh, Mark, really? With company in the house?" his mother asked.

"But hiring a Bow Street Runner is all the fashion now. Soon you will be boasting to your friends about it."

"Now you are putting me on."

"I am for bed," Caroline said. "Thank you, thank you all, for a wonderful evening."

After she left, Thomas said to Lady Cahill, "We have things to discuss."

Roslyn looked up. "Oh, should I excuse myself?"

Mark placed a hand on her shoulder. "I have no intention of leaving you out of our investigations at this point."

"So you found out," his mother said. "Thomas is too clever by far."

"Found out what?" Roslyn asked.

"Mark is not really Lord Cahill," Elizabeth replied.

Thomas dropped his glass and it thunked onto the floor.

"Who is he, then?" Roslyn asked.

"My son," his mother answered. "His father was a kind and handsome naval officer."

"Now a shipping master. In Boston, right?" Mark asked.

"How did you figure it out? Was he too kind and helpful?"

"He was that, and more than once I wished he were my father."

"That's why it is so important for Caroline to have a son," Thomas concluded.

Lady Cahill smiled. "I knew Thomas would run across the connection to himself if he researched long enough, but he never suspected Mark was illegitimate."

Mark smiled proudly.

Thomas choked out a laugh. "No, I did not. I was raised by a distant relative on the maternal side of the family."

"Correct, my son. As Luther was turning into the little monster my husband wanted him to be, I could not stomach giving him another child to ruin."

Mark cleared his throat. "So you turned to the handsome sea captain…and he is still handsome." Mark came and took her hand.

"John suspected you were not his but could not prove it, though he could prevent it happening again only by making me a prisoner."

Thomas said, "But the captain came to you next time?"

"Yes. You are not Lord Cahill either. I feared my husband would kill you or all of us, so I got my sister to come and take me off to Harrogate for the birthing. Do you recall going there, Mark?"

"No but I would have been, what, two?"

"She took the babe and promised to find a safe home for him, a place where my husband could never find him. I'm so sorry, Thomas. It was the best I could do for you."

He sat beside her.

"So we are full brothers," Mark said.

Thomas sighed. "I have always had the best of everything: schools, tutors. And now I have you back."

"I worried less about my son that John did not know about than the one he did. As soon as possible I sent you away, Mark, so he would not kill you."

"You sent me to the right place."

Vincent swiped a hand over his face. "You are brothers, but how did you come together again?"

"We were sent to the same school, and why would I not hire my best friend, hoping to make him my partner?"

"So all is well," Roslyn said, looking around at everyone with a surprised smile.

"Unless Caroline has a girl," Vincent said.

Lady Cahill groaned. "Oh, do not remind me."

## Chapter Thirteen

They all rode together as usual the next day, except Mark ordered a Bow Street Runner to follow in a gig and notice if anyone was spying on them. The man reported nothing unusual, but Mark had not expected trouble in broad daylight.

When they returned, his mother said Caroline had slept late, then asked for lunch in her room. Roslyn looked thoughtful.

"Is something amiss?" Mark asked at luncheon.

Roslyn shook her head. "There is still a week till the baby is due, but Tess came early. Still, I think we are prepared."

"I hope last night was not too much for Caroline," his mother replied.

"With horses, the date can vary by a month either way," Mark said as he took a forkful of the fish he had been served. Everyone looked at him as though he were speaking in tongues.

Vincent laughed. "I doubt Caroline will keep us in suspense that long."

"I want to stay here," Thomas said, "but there is so much to take care of at the office."

"Give me your list," Mark suggested. "You deserve some time off. I can take care of these things."

"I am coming with you," Vincent said.

Mark was about to say he did not need a watchdog,

but he was pleased Vincent was taking an interest in the business and had already started to make plans for recruiting him.

"I am no good at waiting. Perhaps I can help at the warehouse."

Mark nodded. Still experiencing some pain from the last attack, he let Vincent drive. Once again no one seemed to follow or notice them.

When they returned hours later, it was to scurrying servants and a businesslike Roslyn. "She is in labor,"

"I should go for her doctor." Vincent put his hat back on.

"Thomas already went, with one of the Runners."

"What if they do not come back in time?" Mark asked.

Roslyn shrugged. "It will be all right. I was the only one there when Tess was born."

"Really?" Mark asked.

"I did not know that," Vincent said. He hugged Roslyn. "Command me with any task."

"All is under control except the sex of the babe, and none of us can control that."

After two hours by the clock, Vincent and Mark must have passed each other pacing in the upstairs hall for the thousandth time when a kitchen maid brought more hot water and Roslyn came out of the bedroom.

"Thomas not back yet?"

"What can we do?"

"Could you two pace someplace where you do not get in the way, and do not make so much noise, and do not collide with one another."

She took the pail of water from the girl and went back in.

"I guess we have had our marching orders," Vincent said as he started down the stairs.

"Tess is having lessons in the library, so it's either the drawing room or the hall."

Vincent turned to him. "I am just wondering if I should drive somewhere and find a different doctor."

"Come to think of it, why is Thomas not back? The fellow could not have been that hard to find."

Mark hunted up the addresses of the practitioners his mother had collected rather than disturb her in the birthing chamber. He had just handed it to Vincent when they heard a mewing from above them.

"Must be Tess's cat." He pulled his watch out again to calculate how long Thomas had been gone.

After a minute they heard light footsteps on the stairs and saw Roslyn, who stopped when she noticed them.

"It is a girl." She disappeared so fast the men could do nothing but gape at each other.

Mark smiled. "And I am sure she will be as pretty as Tess."

"What do we do now?" Vincent asked.

"I am not going to play Lord Cahill the rest of my life. We shall tell the truth and let the title go into abeyance. The entail cannot be worth much."

"But I have sent Cargill to take care of Glassmere."

"Oh, then I may have to keep up the ruse. There are many titled men who are not actual sons in the line."

The patter of footsteps sounded again in the upstairs hall. When Roslyn saw them loitering at the foot of the steps, she said, "It is a boy." Rosyln was gone again and the upstairs door closed.

They looked at each other and shook their heads.

"Is it that hard to tell?" Mark asked.

"With puppies and kittens maybe, but I thought babies were pretty distinct."

"At least this means there is a new Lord Cahill."

Vincent blew out a tired breath. "We should have a drink or something. My nerves are shattered."

They went to the library and told Tess she had a brother. Once the child ran out, with her governess following, they downed a brandy each, then went back to the hall.

After another ten minutes Roslyn opened the door. "You may come up now."

They mounted the stairs together. His mother was proudly holding a baby, but Caroline was holding one as well.

Mark staggered on the door sill. "Twins?"

Vincent started laughing. "I forgot to tell you twins run in the family."

"What did you think I meant?" Roslyn asked.

Mark clapped his hands together. "This is wonderful."

Caroline looked tired but lovely.

"So you have been cut out of the title after all," Vincent said.

"Thanks be. Have you names for them?"

"I am too tired to think right now and glad the doctor never arrived. He made me nervous."

"What happened to Thomas?" Roslyn asked.

"We shall find him," Mark vowed.

They were going down the back steps when the gig, driven raggedly by Thomas, pulled into the yard. He slid out, turned the reins over to a groom, and helped the Runner to the ground. Mark and Vincent rushed to the man's aid.

"We were attacked coming away from the concert where the physician was supposed to be. If not for Davis, I would have been killed."

"Let's get him inside," Vincent said.

"Ned, go for the doctor you got for John. At least he will come." Mark held the Runner's other arm as they guided him up the outside steps. "To the sofa in the library."

Thomas limped after them. "I do not know why anyone would attack me."

"Because you look like me."

"Oh, right."

Once they got inside, it was obvious Thomas had been mauled as well. He had a cut on his forehead and a bruised knee. Roslyn was kept busy treating both of them until the doctor arrived.

"Well, what about Caroline?" Thomas asked impatiently.

"The proud mother of a girl," Mark said.

"Do not tease him," Roslyn said as she mopped the blood off Thomas's brow. "Caroline had twins, and the second to arrive is a boy."

"And I missed it."

Mark and Vincent looked at each other. "Frankly, I would rather be mauled by an assassin than go through that again."

"Oh, really?" Roslyn asked. "Davis has a broken arm. I doubt you would enjoy that."

Vincent turned to Mark. "We need more Runners."

Chapter Fourteen

Since it rained early next morning and Thomas was still recovering, between visits to gaze at his soon-to-be wife and children, Mark rode to the warehouse to take care of business and pick up the mail. As usual, some personal mail turned up there. He walked into the breakfast parlor later, sorting it. Only Vincent and Thomas were there, having coffee, ham, and eggs.

"You went to the warehouse alone?" Vincent asked.

"Since Roslyn accounted for one assailant and Thomas gave the other some punishment, I thought we might have some leeway."

"Assuming there are only two of them," Vincent corrected.

"Oh, right. Here is business mail, a few invitations for Mother, and one letter for me from the magistrate near Glassmere."

"Why am I getting all the business mail?" Thomas asked as he took up his knife to use for an opener.

"And here is one for the estate. You should open that, Vincent."

Mark cracked open the one from the magistrate.

"What is it?" Thomas asked. "Your face looks awful."

Mark handed the letter to Vincent, who read it and announced, "Someone found a bottle labeled Arsenic in the stream that runs past the house. They want to know

130

if we have any idea where the bottle came from."

"That is pretty cheeky," said Thomas.

Roslyn came in then, and they all stared at her as she got herself tea and a muffin.

She took a bite, then realized they were waiting for her to speak. "Drop the other shoe. What has happened now?" she asked.

"The magistrate says someone found an arsenic bottle downstream from the house and turned it over to him."

"Oh, that must be the one I threw away."

"You?" her brother asked.

"Caroline asked me to buy some."

"Why, in God's name?" her brother asked.

"I did not really buy any." She went back for eggs and busied herself buttering some toast. When she sat down, she finally answered. "I just took an old medicine bottle and labeled it Arsenic. All it had in it was salt, sugar, and corn flour."

"How clever," Mark said. "But why would she want arsenic, and why would you humor her?"

"I think I know." Vincent groaned.

Roslyn swallowed and cleared her throat. "If things got too awful for her to bear, she was going to take it. I was supposed to flee with Tess. Once she knew she was pregnant, she forgot all about the idea."

"How desperate," Mark said in awe.

Thomas looked up. "Don't you see? Having an escape, even such an escape, made her life bearable, gave her back some power."

Mark came and laid his hand on Roslyn's shoulder. He felt her tremble a little. "You had to make sure she never got that desperate."

"I could handle Luther most of the time. I threatened him and even cut him once."

"Good girl," Vincent mumbled.

"So you left the bottle behind? That does not seem like you," Mark said.

"But I did not. I found it when we were packing, dumped it out, and tossed it in the stream. I am surprised anyone could read the writing on the label so much later."

"Or, it is not the same bottle," Thomas supplied.

Mark growled. "I am drafting a reply. How does this sound? *We know nothing about this. I suggest you go to the person who found it and get particulars. Also visit the local apothecary. Possibly if the person who supplied the bottle travels to London, as Hardwick does, you may have to cast a wider net for apothecaries.*"

"Ah. An accusation without it being open. Clever." Thomas went back to slicing open mail with his butter knife.

Mark stopped loading his plate and came back to the table. "Vincent, you are looking flummoxed."

"That was such a facer, and in contrast to the happy news from the Runner we sent to Bath."

"What happy news?" Roslyn asked.

"Our aunt was not a penniless spinster when she took our improvident parents in. She owned a block of houses in Bath and has left the three of us the lot, along with money in funds."

"How could none of you have known that?" asked Thomas.

"Because Hardwick collected the post." Roslyn pushed her plate aside. "Luther may not have even known, or you can bet he would have acted on it."

"We need to tell Caroline," Thomas said.

"Yes, by all means," Mark said with relief.

Vincent stood. "I shall give her the letter. We may all have to go to Bath to sign papers, but there is no hurry for that. What is it, Roslyn? Now you look stunned."

"I do not know. This should be such welcome news, but it just makes me angry."

"Because it was withheld from you by Hardwick?" Vincent asked.

"That too, but there is something else I cannot define."

Mark reached his hand to cover hers. "It cheapens all your sacrifice, knowing now that it was unnecessary."

"Yes. We could have escaped at any time."

Mark shook his head. "If Luther had known of it, he would never have let Caroline and Tess go."

"You are right."

"Vincent looked at her with kind eyes. "And you would never have abandoned her."

"Of course not."

Vincent took a shuddering breath. "This is my fault. *I* should have known about it."

"How could they notify you? You had not even an address. I must go up now."

After Roslyn left, Thomas stared after her. "We have two nursery maids. Roslyn does not have to help so much."

"No, she needs to be with the babies and Caroline now," Mark said. "It is the one place she feels she belongs. The gift of an independence may weigh on her more than the lack of one."

"It will not weigh on me," Vincent said. "To quote you, money should be used for something. I can take care of her now."

"But will she let you?" Mark asked.

"More to the point, will she let you?"

"This would be a dangerous time for me to raise the question, but at least she has the means to make a choice that is not desperate."

\*\*\*\*

Though the twins were asleep and Caroline was reading, Roslyn sat in the room anyway and watched their innocent faces.

Caroline laid her book aside. "Thomas asked me to marry him yesterday, and I accepted."

"I am happy for you. And glad he asked you yesterday."

Caroline looked up at her. "What an odd thing to say."

"Vincent just got a report from the Runner sent to Bath. The executors of our distant aunt have been trying to reach us. She has left the three of us a row of houses and money in funds. How much, I do not know."

Caroline stared at her as if she might be joking.

"I know. It is almost a slap in the face after what we have endured. Apparently, our father is dead and we are the last heirs."

"But how long has it been since Aunt Sadie died, and why? Oh, the mail."

"Yes, Hardwick withheld the news, planning to get his greedy hands on that money as well."

"Luther would have spent it anyway."

"If he had known about it."

"So the estate solicitor was not informed?"

"I had not thought of that. Perhaps he is close with Hardwick. I shall suggest that possibility to Vincent and

Mark."

"It just seems so unfair to have money now that we do not need it so desperately."

"Perhaps that is why I feel so angry."

"Ros, you know anger only hurts you. Forget the inheritance, but it means you do not go to Mark a beggar. You are going to marry him, are you not?"

"Part of me wants to, but not out of gratitude. I hate being rescued."

"If you had a child, you would be glad for a rescue now and then. Being a mother changes your view of life."

"Then I am not sure I want any children."

"Pick up little Vincent or Rose and tell me that."

Roslyn laughed and stared at the sleeping babies. "I cannot deny their appeal."

****

After they finished business for the day, Thomas won the toss to take decisions to the office and Mark made him take a Runner with him, not the one who had been clubbed and was now recovering in an upstairs bedroom.

Mark got out all the papers that had to do with the murder and laid them out on the library table.

Vincent came in and looked over his shoulder. "Thomas's partnership—is it announced yet? I was wondering if it had anything to do with the attack on him."

"No, it is filed and legal, but I am waiting until the refugee family is shipped out."

"Your missing seaman will be lying in wait to see when they are taken to a ship."

"I know, and I do not want Thomas involved when

we trap the slave taker." Mark grinned at him. "Sorry, I just assumed you might want to help."

"I do. Thomas knows about your rescue missions?"

"Yes, but he is a family man now, or soon to be. I am trying to figure out how to keep him safe."

"Simple. Do not make him your agent in this reverse trade."

"No, I was going to continue to take those risks myself."

"Not if you are planning on marrying my other sister. But I would be willing to be your agent in this business now that I have dumped the care of Glassmere on someone else."

Mark slid back the chair to look at him. "It would be extremely dangerous, as you already know."

Vincent shrugged. "I am used to danger. Perhaps I feed on it."

Mark pulled some papers from the desk. "Here is what I had in mind. You will be our trading agent in America, in charge of all cargo of any kind. Then you can keep all safe. I have made a list of safe contacts for you in the port towns. I will give you funds in case you need bribe money."

Vincent started laughing. "You had this all laid out, but you were not going to suggest it to me?"

"I think I know you pretty well by now, but I did not want to dump such danger on anyone I like."

"I am volunteering!" Vincent insisted.

"What if you fall in love with one of my father's attractive daughters?"

"I have a feeling I will not. I am better as a lone wolf."

Mark smiled at this image. "So we just have to stop

this slave taker and find out who hired him."

"You make it sound simple. Will the Runners be any help with this?"

"No, we cannot let them know anything about it. I am pretty sure I am breaking some American laws. Our villains must come to us."

"Yes, we need a foolproof trap."

"Still working on the details of that, but the news from Bath neatly divides our investigation."

Vincent sat on the side chair. "How so?"

Mark gathered up and stacked the sheets for Vincent, then handed them to him. "We now have a solid motive for Hardwick to kill Luther."

"Ah, to keep him from finding out about the inheritance. He would have wanted it for himself. With any luck, Hardwick and his accomplice, the Cahill solicitor, could have divided up the lot."

"I am putting all this in a letter to the magistrate at the village near Glassmere."

Vincent nodded. "It may not be a solid case, but it will stop him thinking one of us did Luther in."

"Exactly. And I can bring more charges against Hardwick. I expect he will implicate the solicitor to save his own hide."

"You do not take his threat to you seriously?"

"Nor Raby's. It is a pistol that can only be fired once. They reveal I am not Lord Cahill, and whether or not anyone believes them, I puff off the birth of our nephew, who has multiple guardians other than me."

"Do you think the family is safe, then?"

"I hope so. We have to act as though we are. Now that we have sent a representative from our law office to Bath, Hardwick can do nothing."

"So we can escort Roslyn to this ball tonight with a quiet mind."

"I nearly forgot about that. At least we should act as though we have quiet minds."

****

Roslyn got out of the carriage and looked down at her brand-new dancing slippers and her newest gown made of the ice-blue satin she had so admired. She was careful to avoid a puddle as Vincent took her arm and helped her toward the steps of the brightly lit mansion.

"Why must I go to this ball? I scarcely know anyone."

"Because Mother says you should." Mark followed, making sure no passing carriage splashed her. "She and Caroline were invited as well."

Vincent laughed. "But it is more fun to stay home and play with the babies. Seriously, Ros, you will never get to know people if you do not go about."

"I feel uncomfortable leaving Caroline home alone," she said as they mounted the stairs to form part of a line waiting to get in.

Mark counted on his fingers. "She has Thomas, two nursery maids, the new governess, Tess, and Mother, not to mention all the servants and the Runner stationed in the house."

"I know. They make me feel so unnecessary."

Her brother took her hand as they waited in the receiving line. "The problem is, Ros, you have been far too necessary to everyone your whole life. You have nothing of your own. No friends or confidantes, no one to gossip with."

"As if I would."

Mark smiled at her. "And you are too serious.

Tonight is for fun."

"I am not used to being happy."

Vincent grinned. "We shall have to change that."

They were so long in the receiving line that sets were forming up when they got to the ballroom. As agreed, Vincent stood up with Roslyn first, and Mark went to offer apologies to Elizabeth's cronies and to inform them she was absent because of her two new grandchildren. All of them exclaimed in delight and promised to call when Caroline was ready to receive visitors. Mark calculated that news would spread like wildfire and stomp out any gossip about his heritage.

He enjoyed watching Roslyn and Vincent dance more than he would have liked to dance with her himself. He could study her face this way, and she did look happier than he had ever seen her.

After that, she was bespoke for every dance, and Vincent watched over her while Mark toured the refreshment salon to spread the news about the new heir among the gentlemen. He wanted Lord Raby to hear about it as soon as possible.

It pleased them that Roslyn went in to supper on the arm of a young lord of impeccable lineage. Well, it did not really please Mark, but he wanted her to have a choice of other men. He and Vincent did not bother to eat but stood within sight of her and within hearing of her laughter. There would be more dancing afterward, and Mark wanted her to take all the joy in the evening that was possible.

"You have been conspicuous by your lack of attention to Ros."

"I was trying to stay out of the way. Did she meet anyone we do not like?"

"Only Raby, but I got rid of him."

Mark emptied his champagne glass. "You did not kill him or anything, did you?"

"I did not even strangle him as you would have. But I caught part of their conversation, and he knows."

"About the inheritance? That proves he was in Hardwick's confidence."

"Yes, the rest of them simply like her because they like her and her skill at the pianoforte. She may have been roped into more musicales."

"I think she will enjoy that, and it is less dangerous than a ball."

"Roslyn spent a great deal of time scanning the crowd for you."

"Like a coward, I was dodging agile misses and their mamas, trying to avoid entanglement. I even produced a temporary limp that I thought credible."

"So was I dodging entanglements, but with more ingenuity."

"You are being hunted as well?" Mark asked.

"You would not think a row of houses in Bath and some money in funds would make me a target."

"So everyone knows, but how?"

"Probably Raby after I threatened him. He was drunk. Never could hold his liquor or his tongue."

Roslyn came out and grabbed her brother by his sleeve. "Could we go home now?"

"Is something wrong?" Mark asked.

"Too much champagne. My head is spinning."

In the carriage, she sighed heavily and rested against the seat.

"So how did you enjoy the evening?" Mark asked.

"Sadly boring."

"Why?" Vincent sounded surprised.

"The young men have no conversation and the misses have insipid conversation."

Mark laughed. "Marry me. You will never be bored again."

"No, I will be worried to death."

"I remain in England. You should be worried about Vincent, who will now leap on the foreign adventures like a dog on a bone."

She looked at her brother with the hint of a smile. "You need that, just as I need—"

"What?" Mark asked. "To take care of someone? Lord knows I need a keeper."

"The problem is I do not know what I need."

"But what do you *want*?" Mark insisted.

"I have never permitted myself to think about it."

"Now is your chance."

Just as they got out of the carriage at home and were about to go in, one of the grooms came out of the stable with a huddled figure.

"M'lord, this girl was hiding in the stable. She says she knows the family."

The girl pulled the hood of her cloak back with one hand. The other arm held a bundle.

"Molly! How ever did you get here?" Roslyn asked.

"I walked."

"From Glassmere?"

"No, I took a stage. I was looking for Steven. But London is so big…and I was with child…" She burst into tears, and Roslyn looked at the bundle she carried, then swept off her cloak and bundled Molly in it.

A mewing sound convinced Mark it was a baby Molly held.

"Let me guess," Vincent said. "They took you to Magdalen Hospital."

"Yes, but they wanted to keep my babe to adopt him out."

"You did well to find us. You are a courageous girl," Mark said.

Roslyn hugged her. "I shall find you something to eat in the kitchen, and Cook will make a room for you upstairs."

"Molly, you work here now, when you are able," Mark assured her. "You can attach yourself to either my mother's household or Lady Caroline's."

"Thank you, sir."

Roslyn led the girl up the steps slowly, though her own fatigue must have been great.

Once the men were inside, the butler secured the door and Mark and Vincent went to the library for brandy. Within half an hour Roslyn joined them.

"She was hungry and is nursing the baby now. Cook is a pushover for infants. Molly has named her son Steven after his father. Steven was the blacksmith's assistant to her father."

Vincent emptied his glass. "I assume her father drove him away before he knew she was with child."

"Molly thinks if she can find Steven he will marry her."

Mark shrugged. "I will put the Runners onto it tomorrow. I feel better and better."

"About what?" Vincent asked.

"About Luther. The baby is not his. Whatever else he is guilty of, he is not guilty of that."

Roslyn glared at him. "Not for want of trying. I thought she ran away to escape his advances."

"Oh, well, at least we know what you are going to do with your life now."

"What?"

"You are going into the rescue business." Mark pulled a roll of paper out of the bookshelves and spread it on the desk. "I have nine lots here, an acre each, and we sit in the middle of them. You can set up your own foundling home, a weaving shop to employ the girls, a truck garden to feed them, and anything else you can think of."

"Are you being funny?" she demanded.

"I am completely serious."

"You had better be, since I might just take you up on that offer."

Roslyn went out the door, then poked her head back in. "I did not want to question her now, but it is possible Molly knows something of Luther's death, since that is when she disappeared."

Mark sighed. "We will deal with that later."

She smiled. "Another babe to take care of. I begin to feel very domestic." She left with a smile on her face again.

Vincent stood and rubbed his forehead. "There will not be as much competition to take care of Molly's child."

"Just the rest of the kitchen staff who are not nursery maids. Still, Roslyn can put herself in charge. She will love that."

"Is that really what she needs, to run a charitable institution?"

"She is a powerful woman who has lived with constraint too long. She needs an outlet. I plan to make that path easy for her."

"But then she might not marry you."

"Or she might marry me someday. Right now she would not."

Vincent nodded and left the door open as they climbed the steps to the room he occupied here when it was too late to go to the town house. He did not often go back to the town house except to pick up clean gear. Like Roslyn, he was still on guard and would never relax, possibly not even when all was made safe.

If they could trap the slave taker, that would help, but if they captured him, what were they to do with him? There could be only one answer, and Mark did not like it. But he was going to use himself as bait, so likely it would come down to self-defense, either successful or not.

Chapter Fifteen

Mark got Vincent to agree to guard the house while he rode to work and spent the entire day at the warehouse office and dock, making all ready for the rescued family to ship out. Also making a target of himself. He gave the family enough silver to see to their needs once they landed on their home continent. He personally thought they would be safer in Canada or England and had offered to find them lodgings and work, but that would only be safer if they could catch the dog who was pursuing them. It was nearly dark when he left, warning the two guards that no one must be allowed to get near the warehouse.

Mark smelled smoke when he rode into the stable yard. The traveling carriage was just leaving, so he was torn. There was so much chaos with grooms carrying water from the well to the house and apparently dumping it down a cellar window, he just pushed his horse into a stall and ran for the house. When he rushed in, he saw that the windows had been opened and that a dribble of blood drops led down the hallway. Mark burst into the library to find Vincent sipping a brandy while Roslyn tied up his shoulder.

"Thank you, my dear, you are better than an army surgeon," her brother said.

"Where is everyone? I saw the carriage headed north."

"Sorry to give you a start," Vincent said. "Only as far as the town house. Caroline, Tess, and the babies should be safe there with Thomas and one Runner to guard them, along with my man."

"I thought we were well prepared for an attack on the house."

"So did I, unfortunately."

"What happened?"

Roslyn cleared her throat, and for the first time he saw the blood on her buff muslin gown and smudges of smoke on her face.

Vincent took another sip. "Someone broke a downstairs window and started a fire in a storeroom. If not for the Runner, it might have taken hold. He smelled the smoke first."

"Is there any reason someone would want to burn your house down?" Roslyn asked.

"Only to empty it," Vincent said.

"What are you not telling me?" she asked calmly.

Mark sighed and leaned on the desk. "For several years now I have been aiding runaway slaves to get back home or to any other country where they would be safe and welcome."

She stared at him. "And you rescued some this time?"

"A family. They are still at the warehouse."

"It would be harder to burn the warehouse," Vincent said. "The owner hired a slave taker."

Roslyn looked confused. "This can have nothing to do with your brother's murder."

"No, but it may be why someone has been trying to kill me."

Vincent chuckled. "There can always be more than

one crime and certainly more than one villain. He started the fire in the storeroom because this is where he thought they were hiding."

"And you tried to stop him." Mark glanced at the bloody shirt sleeve.

"I had almost caught him in the stable yard when he shot me. I should have had a loaded pistol by me. I will not make that mistake again."

Mark groaned. "He now knows they are not here and will try the warehouse. I must go back and warn the guards."

"Now that he knows they are not here, he will not burn the warehouse. He gets no fee if he kills them. He will try to find them there or on the other ship in the harbor."

"We almost moved them today, but there was too much activity on the dock."

"We had better go." Vincent stood, discarded the sling Roslyn had fashioned, and slid his jacket back on.

"But you are wounded," Roslyn protested.

"Makes no great matter. It is almost a comfortable feeling at this stage in my life. I am more used to it than to feeling well."

"I am going with you," Roslyn said.

"I had rather you kept charge of the servants here." Mark knew she would see through this.

She surprised him by saying, "Very well."

"Could you send word to the grooms we need a team hitched to the landau?"

"Of course."

Mark unlocked the gun cabinet in the library and took out two brace of pistols. He began loading one and Vincent the other. "You can keep one of these pair, which ever you like."

"I fancy these heavy ones."

Roslyn sighed her exasperation and removed the bowl of bloody water when she left on her errand.

When they had each lodged a pistol in a waistband and one in a coat pocket, the men loped down the back steps, and Mark told the grooms he would drive. No need for unwanted witnesses.

Once onto the roadway, Mark lashed the team into a cantor. "If there is only one of him, I can take him myself."

Vincent just stared at him.

"Or I could get some of the crew from the two ships in harbor."

"But then too many would know about your clandestine operation, and we may have to eliminate the slave taker in a way that could end with us explaining ourselves in court."

"I thought you were going to say with us getting hung."

"Certainly not a lord of the realm, even a displaced lord."

****

Roslyn methodically cleaned the blood out of the hall and disposed of all signs of carnage, including covering her ravaged skirt with a clean apron. Though the cook was still weeping, the other servants had made sure the fire was out and were mopping up the mess.

Roslyn checked and found Molly had not left the house but huddled in her room, convinced her angry father had found her and set the fire to be rid of her. Roslyn assured her that was not the case and took her some soup.

Roslyn was now pacing the drawing room, and looking out the window. When she heard the front door click open, she was surprised no one had remembered to lock it. What if it was Raby—or worse, this slave taker they spoke of? She stepped out of the way of the light and slipped behind a window hanging. A tall man slunk into the room.

There were two men, and she hoped they could not hear her heart thudding against her chest where she stood behind the hangings.

"No one here. All still downstairs." It was a high voice, cultured, a voice she recognized from the party she had just attended. Lord Korbin, she recalled. She also recognized the sniff before each statement as though he had been taking snuff.

"Must all be dealing with the damage," said a heavier voice with an accent.

"You watched the house? No one crept away?"

"No, they could not have been here."

"The warehouse, then."

She held her breath and did not move for a moment even after she heard the front door click shut. Then she grabbed her cloak and ran down the front steps. Their carriage was well down Blue Anchor Road before she could stop a hackney. No doubt it had been headed for the theaters to pick up fares.

She told the driver someone was ill so she had to hurry to St. Savior's dock. When they got half a block short of the brick building, she paid him from the coins in her pocket and sent him off. She did not see anyone about, not even a guard, when she came to the side door. It was unlocked, which seemed damned careless of someone.

Roslyn knew better than to start shouting for anyone. That might get them all killed. If she could, she had to find the freed slaves and get them away. But wouldn't that be what Mark would think of first?

There was a new moon, and few windows to let in what little light it gave. She would be able to see nothing in the cellars, but Mark would have them staying some place with air and light. She started to climb without noise. She was hearing scuffling from the third floor so kept going upward. The rummaging noises were coming from the right of the central stair, so she went left. A hand clamped over her mouth and Mark whispered, "Do not scream." He slowly released her.

"As if I would," she whispered. "Where is Vincent?"

"Escorting our guests to the outbound ship."

"So I am not needed."

"I—we will have to delay these men. The ship cannot up anchor until the morning tide."

"No, we will have to stop them. One of these is Lord Korbin. They came to the house. They actually came in."

"What brass. He must have a plantation in the Carolinas."

"But slavery is illegal."

"In England."

They heard voices coming toward them.

"We must check the ships," Korbin said. "Shoot anyone who tries to prevent us. There will not be many men on board until they are ready to sail."

"Stay here," Mark whispered. "I am going to set a trap for them. When they come my way, escape down the stairs."

"Where are you going?"

"Out that door."

"But it is a sheer drop to the courtyard below."

"There is a rope winch. I will be fine."

Mark made some noise crossing the floor, and more when unlocking the double door through which goods were winched in and out.

"Must be another guard," Korbin said. "Get him."

The door swung open, and she heard the squeak of a block and tackle. That noise meant Mark had grabbed the rope.

The two men rushed the opening, and one screamed as he fell. She ran forward to make sure Mark was safe. Korbin teetered on the edge, grasping the open door, and pulled himself back in.

"You?" He drew his pistol and aimed it at her.

She reached for any weapon she could grab and came up with a spade. She had often wondered what she would do if confronted with such a situation again. When he cocked the pistol, she rushed him and hit him in the stomach. He went off the edge, and the spade clattered to the paving stones with him. She looked out and Mark was standing there staring at the crumpled forms. She rushed down the stairs and came up with him just as Vincent drove back with the landau.

"What happened?" Vincent asked.

Mark shrugged. "They broke in and must have mistaken the bay doors for a storage room."

"Hah. We could not have hoped for anything better." He threw the reins to Mark and got down to check the men. "Both dead. Who is he?"

"Lord Korbin," Roslyn said. "He was at the ball last night, then came to the house tonight while everyone was still in the basement. That's why I came to warn you."

Vincent came to hug her. "He would have killed you,

both of you. Forget you know who he is."

"We should call someone," Roslyn said, wondering if she should tell the truth about what had happened.

"What about your guards?" Vincent asked.

"Yes, Loftus and a lad. I hope they have not killed them. Take Roslyn home and I will search."

"We are not leaving you," she said.

Vincent took her arm. "Ros, I need you to get in and keep the horses steady while I help look. We may be carrying wounded."

They found the guard inside the back door and both helped him up, but he said the lump on his head was nothing. The lad standing watch with him had been hiding under a bench.

When they all came back out, Roslyn said nothing.

Mark helped Vincent into the carriage, since her brother was looking pale. Mark turned to Loftus. "Vincent was wounded when they tried to burn the house, so he insisted we check the warehouse, and he was right."

"Lucky chance. I will send Gilly for the watch. Break into our warehouse, will they? Serves them right. You should all go home. If they need you to give evidence, they will call on you tomorrow. Oh, our passengers?"

"Safe on board the *Camille*."

"Good, good."

They returned to the house with Mark driving. All now seemed quiet. The stable lads turned out to put the team away, and they went in the back door. When Vincent staggered a bit on the steps, Mark put a shoulder under his arm to help him to the library.

"Your wound has broken open," Roslyn said.

"What is a little more claret?"

"To bed with you as soon as I bind this up again."

"First we must get our stories straight." Mark poured Vincent a brandy, then one for himself and one for Roslyn as well.

She actually took a sip of it and felt better, more courageous than before. What use was that now the emergency was over? She also felt relief. Surely those two men were the only real danger left to them. While she bandaged Vincent, they planned to tell the magistrate that the attack at the house in which Vincent was wounded prompted him to insist they check on the warehouse. She went along because of his wound. They found the dead bodies of the thieves who had fallen out the highest loft door.

"What about the spade?" Vincent asked.

Mark looked at Roslyn. "They must have been using it to pry on the lock."

"Perfect. Now if someone can pour me another brandy, I will stagger upstairs and go to sleep."

Once they got Vincent to bed, Mark took Roslyn to the kitchen for some tea. As he hoped, the fireplace was banked but a kettle of water remained hot. While he went about these simple tasks, she got out cups and tea. They could hear Cook and the footmen in the storerooms, separating damaged foodstuffs from good, a task that could have waited till morning if they were not so devoted. At least it kept Cook from weeping.

Mark poured hot water on the leaves. "I would never have asked him to drive the carriage had I realized how serious his wound is."

She sniffed the aroma of the brewing tea. "Vincent would call it superficial."

"You were just in time."

"You are not going to berate me for coming? You needed to know who you were dealing with and that you were ahead of them."

"Yes, it worked out perfectly because of you."

She bit her lip. "And it is not as though I never killed someone before."

He sat and put a hand over hers. She realized then how hers was trembling. Mark's touch stilled that.

"I was the one who pushed my rapist out of the loft, not Vincent."

"I surmised that. Well done in both cases."

"I am a murderer."

"You are formidable, and you were acting in self-defense. Also, you are a purveyor of justice. Do you want something to eat?" he asked as he poured the tea into cups.

"Too much bother. This is fine." She felt amazed he could take her confession so calmly.

They carried their tea to the library and were sitting together with the list of suspects for his brother's murder in front of them once more when the captain of the watch arrived and a footman came up from the basement to let him in.

"The guard at the warehouse said to wait for morning, but we must know what to do with the bodies. They are your seamen?"

"One of them. The tall one, Rollins, was newly employed. He must have thought we kept valuables in there. I do not know what they expected to carry off from a warehouse full of cloth, tinware, and rum."

"His neck was broken. You do not know the other man? His head was smashed in."

Mark saw Roslyn shudder a bit.

"No. Perhaps a hireling?"

"Can you pay for the burial of the seaman?"

"Yes, of course. We are talking about a pauper's grave. The other one as well."

"Very generous of you, sir. Where is the other witness?"

"My brother was wounded but is resting. You could see him tomorrow."

"Probably no need. Good night to you both." He saluted as he left.

Mark turned to her. "You should go to bed and not let this weigh on you."

It was kindly said, and Roslyn managed a weak smile for Mark. "Good advice for both of us."

"Try to forget tonight." Mark hugged Roslyn. "What have I gotten you into?"

"The greatest adventure of my life." She kissed him on the cheek.

"I know you have been braver than this before when you faced down Luther on your own with no hope of help or rescue."

"And no handy Thomas to carry the family to safety."

"Nor a brother who could easily act for you. Vincent feels badly about that."

She looked up at him and saw a rope burn on his neck. "And worst of all, no Mark."

She kissed him for a longer moment that meant the world to her. When she drew back to look at him, his gaze held admiration, not disgust. His eyes shone with love, not fear, weariness but no regret.

"Mark is a bumbling idiot to have led everyone into

this mess."

"But you mean well," she said with a chuckle.

"Does it weigh on you, what happened tonight?"

"It does not weigh on me at all."

Mark bit his lip. "His family will never know what became of him."

"His family might prefer it that way."

"Finally we know there is someone worse than Luther."

She nodded. "Yes, somehow that makes me feel better about all of it."

She left him and realized she was on the verge of accepting him. He had trusted her competence. It was as simple as that.

Chapter Sixteen

When Mark and Roslyn entered the breakfast parlor the next morning, Vincent was there as usual, without even a sling.

Mark's mother was also present, pouring tea for Vincent and getting him a plate of food to which he did not object.

"I decided I must move to the town house," Vincent said.

"To lend respectability since Thomas is there?" Roslyn asked.

"No, to continue Tess's riding lessons. If anyone knows about the move, it will appear that Caroline was only staying here until the twins were safely delivered. Now she has taken possession of her town house. Of course no one knows she is in residence for the moment, and she will not be entertaining for several reasons anyway."

Mark nodded. "The birth of the babies and the death of her husband."

Vincent cut his ham with his left hand. Mark could see that both Roslyn and his mother wanted to help him. "That was months ago. Her wedding to Thomas will go almost unnoticed until it is accomplished, and then they will go straight to Glassmere for the summer."

Roslyn cleared her throat. "I should inform you that Molly prefers not to return to the estate and would rather remain in London to search for Steven Smith, the father of her son. She wants to work here."

"A job for the Runners?" Vincent asked Mark.

"I have already dispatched Gabby on that hopeless mission," Mark said. "How many blacksmiths do you reckon are in London?"

Vincent sucked in a breath and winced. "Hundreds, and more than a hundred named Smith, but why limit the search to them?"

Roslyn went to get a cup of tea. "He was being trained by Molly's father."

"But he may be working as a groom or any lesser position."

Mark groaned.

"Take out an ad in the paper," Lady Cahill suggested.

"Offer of work for Stephen Smith?" Roslyn asked.

Mark shook his head. "Then we will have a hundred Smiths turning up on the doorstep."

"Oh, very well. Just *Molly wants to know the whereabouts of Steven Smith.*" His mother smiled.

"Will that scare him off?" Vincent asked.

Roslyn laughed. "If that would scare him off, we do not want him. If he cares about Molly, he will come and no one else."

Mark grabbed a stub of pencil from his pocket and wrote in a small notebook. "You two are much better at this than I am. Do you think Caroline will be comfortable at the town house?"

"Yes, since I hired more people and you have lent us some of your staff."

"I prefer no one knows she is there. We have solved only part of our puzzle. There is still Hardwick to deal with."

"You are sure it is him?" his mother asked.

"He is the most likely suspect."

"There's also Raby," Roslyn said. "He knows about our inheritance, so that does give him a motive for getting rid of Luther, who would have tried to get his hands on mine as well as Caroline's."

Mark tossed his knife and fork onto his plate. "I want to kill him so much."

"Mark, be nice," his mother said as she rose and whisked out of the room.

Roslyn went off to encourage Molly to let her write to her mother that she was safe or else write to the vicar so he could tell her mother. Vincent ordered his gear packed, then moved with Mark to the library. They had their heads together over a map of the Americas when Thomas arrived to report that all was well and to confer with them on business matters.

"All safe there?" Vincent asked.

"Your man Evers has made the place a fortress. A mouse could not squeak in without being interrogated. Anything to do before the *Camille* sails?"

"All is in order or the captain would have sent word by now. Vincent is going to take over that part of the business."

Thomas blinked. "We certainly need help there."

"This is how we have been running the rig so far," Mark said. "I will write you a letter of introduction to Father so he knows you are to be trusted."

Vincent scrutinized the map with a hungry look in his eye. "In some ways this is the greatest adventure of all."

"I feel as though I am letting you down." Thomas

stared at the map with a sigh.

Mark clapped him on the shoulder. "Just because Caroline accepted your offer and you get desperately seasick even in the harbor?"

"Yes, and she wants to spend part of the year in the country, a better place to raise the children."

"I will bring you tons of paperwork, just the way you used to bury me," Mark said. "Seems perfect."

"Except I know nothing about farming."

Vincent laughed. "You have an agent for that."

Thomas looked at Mark. "So you remain here."

"Roslyn has *not* accepted my offer. If she means to go with Caroline, it might be too painful for me to go to Glassmere. I cannot be around her without pressing her, and she wants her freedom or something I cannot give her."

The door opened and Roslyn glanced at the three men. "Is Elizabeth in the house?"

"I do not think so. What is the emergency?"

"I wish to consult her about a task I would like Molly to perform. As you know, Molly decided to work for your mother to avoid returning to Glassmere."

"I am sure Mother would not quibble about any work you assigned Molly. What is it? Maybe we can advise you."

"I do not think so."

"Come now. We are resourceful fellows. Ask us?"

"Caroline writes that she fears she will not have enough milk for both babies as they grow, and I need to hire a wet nurse."

Vincent and Thomas both looked surprised.

Mark nodded. "Oh, just ask if Molly is willing to play wet nurse. She has plenty of milk. Someone can drive her up a couple of times a day. I am sure Mother would approve."

"Very well." Roslyn went out, then popped the door open again. "How would you know Molly has plenty of milk?"

Mark gaped at her, unable to think of an answer.

She sent him a withering look. "Never mind." She then slammed the door after her.

Vincent held his laughter in, but Thomas rocked in helpless peals. Finally Vincent broke down.

Mark shook his head. "This is what I get for thinking on my feet."

Vincent took a breath. "The answer to your quandary is to make Roslyn jealous."

"Not with Molly. Poor girl has enough problems hoping her beloved will appear. The ad was a good idea, but what if he does not see it?"

"Or cannot read," Thomas added.

"Oh, bother."

Chapter Seventeen

Vincent and Roslyn had a meeting that afternoon with their new estate solicitors, who were also Mark's solicitors. He went along to make introductions and smooth things out. The junior solicitor had returned from Bath and reported that their aunt's will could now be probated and that her solicitors were prepared to turn over the accounts in the funds and the management of the houses. Roslyn looked helplessly at Vincent.

"I do not want to reside in Bath."

"Nor do I," said Vincent.

Mark's solicitor cleared his throat. "Perhaps the Bath firm could continue to manage the properties for the time being. They will notify you when you have to appear there."

"Caroline should be able to travel soon."

On the way home, Roslyn owned to feeling a little different now that the inheritance was actually real. She was not sure she liked having money. She would rather be valued for herself.

When they returned, Molly, red-faced and tearful, ran up to the carriage and grabbed the side before it was well stopped.

"Help, my lord. Someone has taken little Steven."

"Stolen him, you mean?" Mark leaped out.

"I was taking in the dry laundry. The day was so fair I had him in one of the baskets on the lawn. When I looked up, a cloaked figure was running with him. The stable boys are still giving chase. 'Tis the foundling people, I tell you."

"No, I think it is Hardwick, the old agent. He must have been watching the house and thought you were nursemaid to Caroline's babies."

Roslyn saw a scrap of paper on the grass and brought it back to them.

"Is that his writing?" Mark asked.

"Yes, and not very cleverly disguised."

"But how would he know to have a note prepared?" Vincent asked.

"This is not the first day you brought your baby out?"

"No. Any day that is fair I bring him with me when I weed the kitchen garden or pick vegetables."

"Hardwick has been spying on you," Roslyn concluded.

"Ten thousand in silver," Mark said. "That is no problem."

Vincent blinked, then took the note. "Leave it at the paupers cemetery? The first stone on the corner. Gruesome."

"Lord," Molly said, tears streaming down her face. "I don't have a pound, let alone that much."

"But I do. Molly, I will go to the bank and take the money as instructed to the cemetery. I doubt very much that he will have Steven with him when he comes for it. You three take the carriage and go to Hardwick's lodgings."

"What if Steven is not there?" Molly asked.

"I am betting Hardwick will leave him there until he gets the money. The Runners inform me he lodges at the corner of Lampshady Lane and Dodger Way. Take the Runner with you if you can find him. He has been to Soho before. Hunt for the babe. Come back here whether you find him or not. If not, we have the ransom in place. Roslyn, can you go with her?"

"Will you need the barouche, Mark?" Roslyn asked.

"I will harness the curricle. Your errand is more desperate."

"Mark, stop at the town house and get Evers to go with you," Vincent said. "Someone will have to hold the horses when you get to the cemetery."

Roslyn got Molly into the carriage. "We may not be back by the time you have to leave the ransom."

"No matter." Mark ran into the stable and led a horse out himself. Vincent went to help him hitch up a team, but the Runner and two of the grooms came back at that point.

"Have you a loaded pistol in your pocket?"

"I do," Vincent said.

"So do I."

As it turned out, the Runner knew the way intimately and instructed the groom how to go. The narrow streets were full of obstructions, and night folk were emerging by this time. Roslyn realized it would be full dark by the time they got home, whether they found the baby or not, and Mark would be accomplishing his task at night.

When they got to the address, a ramshackle house on a corner, Vincent led the way and pushed open a sticky door. They entered the dim hallway and looked at four closed doors.

An infant squalled somewhere.

"I hear him… My baby! He is crying!"

Roslyn wondered that she could identify Steven, since other infants cried in houses all about them. A worried woman came out of one door and closed it.

"Are you the landlady, and did Mr. Hardwick ask you to keep a child for him?" Roslyn asked.

She nodded. "Says it's 'is nevvy. I don't believe it. Wot's he doin' wit' a suckling babe?"

Molly launched herself toward the door and would have beat it down if it had not opened. She snatched up the weeping infant and bounced it before sitting uninvited in a wobbly chair to let it suckle.

Vincent was reaching for a coin. "Clearly this is the babe's mother. Hardwick stole the child and is now wanted for kidnapping."

"I had nought to do wit' that. The babe idn't even old enough to eat. The man must be mad."

"I will pay for your care of it, if you agree to lay evidence against him."

"For certain I will. He's not paid his shot these three months."

"I will pay that as well. We are taking the babe as soon as he eats."

"Oh, he's wet," Molly said.

Roslyn sent her brother an imploring look.

Vincent sighed and stripped off his stock. "Will this suffice?"

Vincent sent the Runner in a fast hackney to try to catch Mark at his bank while they waited for Molly to feed Steven.

\*\*\*\*

Mark drove the curricle himself. He stopped to send a note to his bank regarding funds needed, then picked up Evers, who seemed eager for action. When they reached the bank, the manager already had the ransom done up in two satchels, a heavy load evenly divided. Then they drove the curricle to the cemetery. It was nearly dark when they stashed the money where instructed, then drove off. They turned a corner and drove back almost to within sight of the grave marker.

"What is your plan?" Evers asked in his rough voice. "To catch the kidnapper?"

"If they bring the babe, to make it safe. If they do not bring it, to follow them."

"Is there more than one man?"

"There must be, if only to hold the horses. This is just in case Vincent and Roslyn do not find the child at Hardwick's lodgings. Whether the kidnapper is Hardwick or not, we must track him. I am going to get a little closer."

"Don't let anyone see you."

They waited in silence with the curricle in shadow in an alley, but it was full dark and no one could have seen it anyway. Mark stood at the corner of a building from which he could see the satchels. A few drunken men wandered down the street singing, followed by a few more. Mark walked over to consult Evers.

"Where are all these fellows going at this hour? I thought the cemetery would be deserted."

"There's a cockfight pit hereabouts. The fights might be ready to start for the night."

"Wonderful."

A gig with two passengers, drawn by a single horse, pulled up at the corner of the cemetery. One man got out and grabbed the valises one at a time, loading them on the back of the gig and strapping them in place while the other man held the reins. Some of the drunken crowd accosted them, asking for money. The driver tried to steer the gig away, but half a dozen fellows blocked its path, and the horse reared.

"Drive over them," Hardwick shouted.

"Damn, what should we do?" Evers asked Mark.

"Hold your peace. They may delay them."

Mark saw a knife flash as the gig indeed drove over the feet of two men. Then he heard the jingle of silver hitting stones as the gig lurched forward, the horse in a panic.

A bigger crowd had formed by now and rushed the gig, but everyone stooped to pick up the coins. The driver whipped up the horse and tore away. Mark leaped into the curricle and followed as best he could without running anyone down, but the trail of silver coins still spilling from the slit valise threatened to bring a mob down on them.

One terrified horse would be no match for his team, but the driver was twisting his way through alleys almost too narrow for the curricle.

Feathering too closely past one desperate corner, the gig caught a wheel and overturned. One man yelled some invective at the thrashing horse, and then, seeing their approach, fled without even attempting to take the other bag of silver.

Mark halted the team and handed the reins to Evers. He examined the driver, who had been thrown clear of the wreckage. "It is Hardwick, and he is dead. A broken neck, I think. I am going to try to save the horse from breaking his leg, then go after the other man. The curricle will never fit down some of these paths. Wait here."

He cut away all the traces but the reins, narrowly avoiding the horse's hooves except for getting stepped on once, and at last threw himself up on the bare back of the frightened beast. They went the direction of the limping man but were soon lost in the stews. He turned the horse and found Evers calmly holding his team.

"We have at least left the mob behind," Mark said.

"Not the safest place to stop, sir. The watch do not even patrol here."

"Let's for home. You can drive the curricle to the town house for the night, and I shall ride this hack home slowly. They all need to be cooled. I will deal with the magistrate in the morning."

"At least I saved one of your bags of silver."

"Did you, by God? Then it is your retirement fund. I just hope the babe is still alive somewhere."

Half an hour later, Mark rode the tired horse into the stable yard and rapped up a groom to take care of the hack.

"M'lord, they found the baby," the head groom said.

"Thank God." Mark rested his head on the withers of the horse, then pulled himself together. "A couple of lads can pick up the curricle and team at the town house tomorrow."

Roslyn opened the back door, and Mark found the energy to limp up the steps.

"Come inside for a brandy. I am certain you need one."

"Are you all right?" he asked as he hugged her and went with her to the library.

"Yes, Molly and the baby went to bed."

Vincent was still up and smiled at sight of him. "He was hungry and wet, to be sure, but they are fine."

"Thank God. It was Hardwick. and he is dead, so we have some cause for relief."

"Did you…?" Roslyn asked.

"Kill him? No. The gig overturned and he broke his neck when he was thrown out. I suppose I should report that. There was someone with him, but he got away."

Vincent nodded. "We will tell our Runner, who will know what to do. Tomorrow. Do we tell them about the kidnapping?"

"I think we have to. There is still the man who ran away from the wreck."

Roslyn sat. "So we are not completely safe yet."

"But getting closer."

"And this time you are not shot?" she said brightly.

"No, I am fine."

"Or stabbed?"

Mark rolled his gaze heavenward as Vincent chuckled.

"But you are limping."

"If you must know, the horse I rescued stepped on my foot."

"Oh, that's all right, then."

\*\*\*\*

The staff served dinner without waiting for them to change, and it was not much ruined for being held an hour. Mark drank too much and stretched out his leg to relieve the pressure on his foot. Why not just admit it hurt?

When he finally retired to his room, Roslyn walked in on Jarvis working his boot off.

"Looks to me as though it could be broken. I will get a poultice," she said.

"Will it be something foul-smelling?" Mark called after her.

"As foul as possible."

She left and he leaned back against his pillows and pulled the stack of paperwork to him. After a smart rap, the door opened and Vincent came in to stare at his foot.

"She says it is broken. Would she know?" Mark asked.

"Roslyn? Probably. Under normal circumstances, seeing my sister flit out of your bedroom might cause me to ask for satisfaction or an immediate wedding."

"No one is more in favor of us marrying than me. I must have asked her twenty times, though I should have consulted you first."

"I have no control over Roslyn, and I do not know her feelings in this matter."

"I do not think she does either, except that she will not abandon her post until Caroline, Tess, and the babies are absolutely safe. Hardwick had an accomplice for the kidnapping, if not for the murder."

"But we may never find him. They may never be safe."

"I know. It is the only reason I care about finding Luther's killer."

"Since things seem to be under control here, I shall go to the town house for the night. Should I tell them of this?"

"Yes, it is unwise to shield Caroline. Another attempt could be made later."

Roslyn pushed the door open with a tray.

What is that smell?"

"Comfrey has no smell, so it is the mustard."

Vincent fanned the air. "I will leave you to it."

Mark submitted to the plaster and had to admit his foot felt better.

"At least it is not your ankle, just a foot bone."

"Thank you for all your care of me. I should not be such a charge on you."

"But I am happy to help. Have I ever said how much I admire you?"

"Me? What have I done except land us in a whirlpool of trouble?"

Roslyn sniffed. "When you read how much they wanted for a ransom of little Steven, you did not even think about it. You went to get the money as though it was little Vincent."

"And why should I value Molly's son less than Caroline's?"

"I agree with you. And I was not surprised. You are just unusual."

"Having not had money and then had some, I can tell you the only good it does is to spend it. Now that you have some to deal with, you will find that out."

"Yes, I see that now. "

She leaned over him and kissed him on the lips in a way that made him forget all about the pain in his foot. But then she left. He cast the paperwork aside and tried to go to sleep.

He supposed this was progress, at least an indication she wanted him as much as he wanted her. But did he have to get injured to awaken her sympathy? And how was he ever going to sleep without a strong dose of brandy?

Then he recalled he had a valet. He rang the bell pull by the bed, and Jarvis appeared within minutes to supply the required brandy. He even thought to bring a cane, one Lady Cahill used when she was feeling stiff. The man was invaluable. Thomas would have to hire his own valet or fend for himself when they separated households.

## Chapter Eighteen

The next day, Mark and Vincent were interviewed by the magistrate about the abduction. Once again the big concern was who would pay for Hardwick's burial. Mark agreed to pay, for old times' sake. They were discussing how to find his accomplice when Roslyn looked in.

"Sorry to interrupt, but what is Raby's hack doing in your stable?"

"Raby?"

"Yes, I recognize it from his visits to Glassmere."

"It's the horse I rescued from the traces last night. Raby must be the man who ran away from the wrecked gig."

"Lord Raby?" the magistrate asked.

"Yes, he keeps turning up here."

"If I try to arrest him for kidnapping, he could say the horse and gig were stolen. And perhaps they were."

"Then we have to trap him," Roslyn said.

"Can't I just confront him?" Mark was already clenching his fists.

Vincent snorted. "We all know how that will end."

Roslyn shook her head. "I know a way. I shall invite him to call."

"Not at this house."

"I will ask him to meet me in the stable so he can retrieve his horse. Properly provoked, he will spit out the truth. You can all hide somewhere within hearing."

"This sounds too dangerous," Mark said. "He could kill you before we could stop him."

"It is dangerous to leave him on the loose"

"Vincent?" Roslyn asked.

"I trust Roslyn to handle him. Magistrate, are you in?"

"I have had many complaints about him but can never get anything to stick. I will be here. Just tell me when."

\*\*\*\*

Roslyn noticed the butler was wary when she and the others had not changed for dinner by late afternoon, and especially as they all paraded out to the stable with the magistrate, Mark limping along in a pair of worn shoes lent him by Jarvis. The staff sensed there was something going on, but they were too polite to ask. They put dinner back, just in case.

Mark put the grooms and coachmen out of danger by giving them the evening off, though Evers stayed. Roslyn passed the time by grooming the hack. It had been fed well and probably treated better in the past day and night than it ever had before. She had a notion to buy it from Raby to make the rest of its life easier.

"So you have finally agreed to marry me."

Raby stepped into the lantern light without the sound of an approaching team. He must have taken a hackney.

"First, I want the truth. Why did you have the baby kidnapped?"

"Kidnapped? What are you talking about?"

She liked the way she disarmed him. "You picked up the ransom from the kidnapping. You were seen running from the carriage wreck."

"No, Hardwick said he was blackmailing Lord Cahill."

"Did it not occur to you it was an odd way to get the extortion money?"

"It did seem strange, but I had nothing to do with any baby."

"In fact, you do not even care about the baby." She was close to swatting him with the curry comb.

"If he stole the heir to the Cahill estate, there is no way to find the child now."

Roslyn shook her head. "You do not see yourself in a moral dilemma, aiding such a man?"

"Hardwick was my friend, just as Luther was."

"And that is why Hardwick told you about my inheritance."

"He had to, or I would have warned Luther he was being swindled by Hardwick."

"I wonder why Hardwick did not warn Luther he was being swindled by you."

"No one can prove a thing," Raby said.

"You do not sound like a friend to anyone."

"When we marry, you will have a title. That is all I offer you."

"As if that would tempt me."

"You will not get one by marrying Mark St. John, now that there is a legitimate heir."

"I have already said a title is no lure. Witness how many times I have rejected your proposals. I always wondered why you wanted me. Now I see my inheritance gave you the perfect motive for killing Luther."

"You stupid girl. You did not even know about it."

"Because Hardwick withheld the information. You had a time limit because you knew eventually we would be contacted."

"You are coming with me now. I have no choice, so you don't either." He grabbed her arm.

"Another abduction?" she sneered.

"I have a hackney waiting. Do not scream, or I will throttle you." He dragged Roslyn toward the stable yard, but the magistrate stepped out.

"I have heard enough. Lord Raby, I arrest you for conspiring to extort money from Lord Cahill and for the attempted abduction of Miss Clary."

Raby drew a pistol. "Get out of my way."

"Let her go," Mark said in unison with Vincent. Raby did not. The pistol he cocked was aimed at Mark's chest.

Roslyn lunged upward with her left hand, and the gun went off. Mark twisted and landed in the straw with a grunt.

The magistrate and the Runner were on Raby at once and quickly trussed his hands.

"And for the attempted murder of Lord Cahill."

"He is probably the one who had the brat abducted," Raby accused. "Then he gets to keep the title."

Mark rolled up on an elbow as Roslyn bent over him. "The title was never mine, the infant Lord Cahill is safe and sound, and Lord Raby has forgotten our conversation on slander."

"Where are you hurt?" Roslyn begged, looking at his head and chest.

"I am not, for once, but just a bit tired and enjoying you so close."

Evers chuckled and reached down one hand to pull Mark to his feet.

"You were right," Vincent said. "It was too

dangerous."

"You cannot arrest me," Raby whined. "I cannot be in jail. They will kill me in there."

"Is that true?" Mark asked the magistrate.

"I have no idea."

After the magistrate left with Raby, they were walking toward the house and thinking of dinner when a stranger in homespun came up to them.

"I would like to see Molly about this notice in the paper."

"I will fetch her," Roslyn said.

"I went to the back door, but the cook shooed me away."

"You are Steven Smith," Mark guessed, then took his hand and shook it.

"Yes, I promised Molly I would send for her when I had enough money together, but it's hard. I have not found work as a smith, so I have been working in the stable at an inn."

"Steven! You came!" Molly ran down the steps and into his arms.

"Of course. You are all right?"

"Yes, and we will not go back home, never. Would you like to see your son?"

"I suspected you were with child. I sent letters."

"Father would not give them to me."

"It will be all right now we're together. I can come see you every Sunday."

"I suggest a more permanent arrangement," Mark said. "Would you like to be a groom here?"

"For certain I would. I could see Molly every day."

"Until we set up a forge. Then you can be our smith."

"This is beyond anything. Thank you so much!" Steven turned to Molly. "Where is the baby?"

Molly led Steven toward the back door.

"They must be married, of course," Roslyn said.

"I am glad you are thinking of marriage." Mark put an arm around her shoulders.

Molly left Steven at the bottom of the house steps and ran back to them. "First I must tell you something. I owe you so much, and I know you are trying to figure out who killed your brother. I think it may have been my fault."

"What?" Mark asked.

"I was leaving the church that night, where I had been praying to get back with Steven. Your brother saw me and chased me. He fell, and I kept running."

"Is that all?" Mark asked.

"Don't you see? He must have hit his head."

"That is not your fault," Roslyn said.

"But I should have gone back to help him. I told my Da, and he said good riddance."

Mark shook his head. "Luther was not well liked, and for many good reasons. I do not blame your father, either."

"When I heard he was dead, I ran away. So will they arrest me?"

"No one is going to arrest you. You were frightened by him. You did nothing wrong. Luther ran to his own death."

Molly nodded, sighed with relief, and went back to a puzzled Steven.

"So, just like that, it is solved," Roslyn said. "Of course, I sent him to the church."

"Do not start. You said Caroline was praying. You

did not make him go to the church." Mark took her hand and entwined his fingers with hers. "It is over."

Vincent blew out a tired breath. "Let us put Luther's demise down to divine retribution and good riddance. Now, am I invited to dinner here or must I go home?"

"Please dine with us," Roslyn said as she grabbed her brother's hand. "We do have much to celebrate. We are completely free of suspects, likely or otherwise."

Roslyn felt a weight lift from her heart. She had not realized how much the fear of seeing her family murdered or kidnapped had been weighing on her until the threat was removed. Now she felt as though she would float away if not anchored to Mark and Vincent by her two hands.

Chapter Nineteen

Molly and Steven were married two weeks after his arrival, and Thomas and Caroline the following day. Mark wondered if the trip to Glassmere would shake Roslyn loose from her sister. After a brief wedding breakfast, they all took the traveling carriage and landau to move everyone to the country for a rest, though they would not all be staying. The servants, except for Molly and Steven, traveled in a hired carriage.

The problem was that Mark did not know who was staying or who was coming home. Vincent would return with him, since the next voyage had been planned. If Roslyn returned to London but not as Mark's wife, then his mother must come home as well.

At Glassmere, Vincent greeted his friend Cargill, who outlined the improvements he had made. As they walked through the house, Mark could tell some of the furniture was new, probably Vincent's work.

After the ladies went upstairs to inspect the bedrooms, Cargill took the men to the wine cellar.

"There is something I want to show you. We had to dump all the bottles of wines made here, though we were able to sterilize the bottles for future use. I am sad to tell you that everything we discarded was contaminated with sugar of lead."

"How would Luther come by sugar of lead?" Thomas asked.

"It is used as a mordant in dyeing fabric. It is sometimes added to wine as a sweetener, but he may not have put it in there on purpose. Let me show you the distilling room." Cargill led them into the other half of the cellar. "The grapes had been pressed with this press, which has lead parts, and left to ferment in this vat, which has lead solder. The acid from the grapes must have reacted with the lead while the grapes were fermenting. Drink enough of it, and you die of lead poisoning."

"Did you ever drink any of that, Vincent?" Thomas asked.

"I should say not," Vincent replied. "That homemade stuff was always foul. I used to bring my own with me."

"So my father murdered himself," Mark said. "How just that he was his own undoing."

"I know your brother died of exposure, but if he had continued to brew wine in this vat, he would have died of lead poisoning soon enough also."

"That may explain the erratic change in his behavior," Vincent said.

"So it was never a mystery at all," Mark said. "Wait till I visit the magistrate."

"Not that kind of mystery anyway," Thomas said.

Vincent smiled. "Best of all, no one need fear for their life anymore."

Mark smiled. "And Glassmere does not seem like such a bad place."

"Shall we join the ladies for dinner?" Cargill asked.

\*\*\*\*

Caroline glowed as she presided over the table, which included Tess and her governess besides the new agent. "We are fixed here until next spring, so everyone who is journeying away is invited for the Christmas holiday."

"I shall be back from America long before then," Vincent said.

"Will you bring me a present?" Tess begged.

"Probably not livestock, but Mark said he promised to replace the chickens and rabbits. We can do that tomorrow."

Tess clapped her hands. She was well dressed and had grown a bit, but she was still excited by anything with fur.

"Will you ever settle down, brother?" Caroline asked.

"I will be the doting uncle who visits often enough to spoil the children, but are you sure you want me to keep the town house?"

"So many of your friends are in London. We may fall in on you for a few weeks in the spring, to shop."

"Roslyn, how about you?" Elizabeth asked.

"I like your house across the river in London. It is almost like the country, with its garden and stable. You made me an offer once?" She turned her gaze at Mark.

The others smiled, probably thinking she meant marriage.

"I did, and it still holds." He nodded.

"An acre to set up a foundling home and school."

Mark cleared his throat. "I think that enterprise might require three acres. The three in the back, to keep all safe. I was thinking a specialty weaving shop to provide the unwed mothers employment, besides the barracks and the school."

"We will discuss it."

"Would you like to take a walk to discuss now a topic that is sure to bore everyone else?"

"Yes, we should have time to get through the matter before tea."

They walked toward the stream, and Mark remembered the old willow. "Tess showed me this little hut under the trailing fronds."

"One of Tess's favorite hiding places. Come inside. We have a bench."

Mark stooped and entered the bower after her. The bench was dry today.

"Seems a comfy hiding place for a child. The grass looks soft. Does it seem less oppressive here now?"

"Yes, now that we can come and go. It was never the estate that cowed us, but the way Luther treated us."

"Like property."

"Exactly. Luther promised me to Raby to compensate him for his gaming debts."

"I am so sorry. I wish I could blame the poison he was drinking for his decisions, but I cannot."

"Vincent did offer to spirit us away."

"But you refused."

"A half-pay officer with three women on his hands, one of them pregnant? Also, I am sure Luther would have sent the law after him if he had tried to rescue Caroline and Tess."

"And you would not leave them."

"Of course not."

Mark stared at her. "Have I ever told you how much I admire *you*?"

"Why?"

"You have never abandoned your post, never had a thought for yourself."

"There are many like me."

"But most at least wish for a life of their own."

"I have a life. I love Caroline, Tess, and the babies. I do not see why we need *two* nursery maids and a governess."

"But the governess is in need of them," Mark pointed out.

"What shame it is to be in need. You rescued all of us."

"You did not need me. We already discussed this. All I did was expedite your rescue of your sister."

"I have to admit your interference was most welcome."

"So you could find other occupations besides caring for Tess and the twins."

"There are many in London and even here who are deserving of help."

"For instance, a home for pregnant girls, with a school to educate their children."

"That would all require my close supervision." She leaned her shoulder against his and turned her head to gaze into his eyes.

"Yes, especially if you set up a weaving business so they can be self-supporting. Let me show you my plan." He drew out a square of paper folded into nine segments. "As I said, the three back acres for the home, the school and the shop. Of course, our house is in the middle, but to the left an acre of vegetable garden to feed your flock, and the stable yard to the right. Then along the road, an orchard, to produce fruit for the flock to sell. The driveway can have flowers planted along both sides. Those are also cash crops in London. And the final square is for Molly's cottage and Steven's forge."

Roslyn took the paper from him. "It is like a little town. You were serious about all this."

"I was a very lonely person for much of my life. I like people about me, lots of them, one in particular." He raised a hand to stroke her cheek.

"You think I should be doing something with my life other than being an aunt."

"Living someone else's life would make you bitter, in the end. Why do you think Caroline hired a governess?"

"To make use of her skills."

"To set you free. You have spent so much of your energy taking care of others you have neglected your own desires."

"I would have to reside in London where you are."

His face fell, and he cleared his throat. "You could do some such thing here where I am not."

"What future would you have for me?" she asked.

"To marry me, of course. I have asked you often enough, but I am not your only choice."

"Which is why you and Vincent have been dragging me to social gatherings, to meet other men."

"Who all fall sadly short of expectations, but it is your life."

"Stop trying to make me laugh. I cannot decide the future in a moment."

"You also have time. I will always be around as a trusty alternative in case you run out of good works."

"Seriously?" She smiled at his desperation.

"Though I really think you could handle both at once."

"I would miss seeing the family every day."

"We would visit often. When not bringing a three-carriage entourage, we could nip up here in under four hours. You can drive."

"You are still a risk taker."

"Vincent has informed me I botched the repatriation of the Africans by making it dangerous, whereas he can run the operation more smoothly and safely."

"I have no doubt of that."

"With Thomas now struggling to learn about farming and cope with his growing family, it looks as though I shall be left in London to keep the books and escort Mother to teas and occasional piano recitals."

"You are a great deal more than a bookkeeper."

She leaned over and put her arms around him, stroking the back of his neck.

"Will you have me?" he asked, even though it stopped her kiss.

"We are not residents of the same parish. It would take some time."

His hand dived into his breast pocket. "I have here a much dog-eared and creased special license, which I have been saving for just such a moment. That is why I dropped to the ground when Raby fired. I was afraid to get blood on it."

Roslyn started laughing so hard she fell off the bench onto the nest of grass at their feet. "No ring?"

"Always in my coat pocket. Can you think of no other obstacle to throw in our path?" He knelt over her.

"None. You have managed everything, as usual, from the moment you first dumped that bag of coins in my lap."

"Never. I dropped it on the table in the wildest fear that you would throw it back in my face."

"I was tempted."

"Which accounts for my hasty exit. I may never make a good entrance, but I do know how and when to exit a room." He slid down beside her on the soft grass.

"And you do know how to make me laugh no matter what absurdity you have gotten into."

He took her hand and placed the ring on the correct finger. "Tomorrow?"

"Unless you have a minister in your pocket somewhere, we shall have to wait."

"Until tomorrow. In the garden," he said. "Then away to where?"

"I would like to visit Bath at least once to make sure our row of houses is not a ruin."

"Then Bristol, and perhaps even Portsmouth and Brighton before we return to London? We can go other places, if you like."

"Bath will be enough for now. You have made me happy."

"And you have made me complete. May we go back to the hall now and end the suspense everyone is suffering?"

"Let us linger for a bit in this perfect bower."

She pulled him to her, and his lips finally drank of her sweetness. He knew it was not a stolen kiss or a stolen moment—she promised him a lifetime.

## A word about the author…

Barbara Jean Miller has mentored in the Writing Popular Fiction Masters Program at Seton Hill University since its inception in 1999. She writes in several genres, but her favorite is historical romantic suspense. She calls them action/adventure romances with the heroine sharing in the struggles and rescue in equal parts with the hero. These struggles often involve mysteries and horses.

Barb lives with her husband and pets on an ancient farm in Western Pennsylvania which contributes authentic settings to her novels.

https://barbarajeanmiller.substack.com

Thank you for purchasing
this publication of The Wild Rose Press, Inc.

For questions or more information
contact us at
info@thewildrosepress.com.

The Wild Rose Press, Inc.